A VOLATILE Range

ANDREW GREY

Dreamspinner Press

Published by
Dreamspinner Press
5032 Capital Circle SW
Ste 2, PMB# 279
Tallahassee, FL 32305-7886
USA
http://www.dreamspinnerpress.com/

A Volatile Range

Cover Art by L.C. Chase
http://www.lcchase.com

ISBN: 978-1-62380-333-9
Digital ISBN: 978-1-62380-334-6

Printed in the United States of America
First Edition
January 2013

Readers love Andrew Grey

An Isolated Range

"…a truly unique story… bringing to mind how fragile and uncertain life can be, reminding us all not to take life and love for granted."

—Literary Nymphs

A Foreign Range

"Mr. Grey is the master at building sexual tension between his characters, but there is always the emotional attachment as well that just makes the romantic in me give a deep and satisfied sigh at the end of his books."

—Guilty Indulgence

A Troubled Range

"This is one book that I won't forget and you shouldn't miss it."

—Fallen Angel Reviews

"…a solid, sweetly romantic and delightful story that will leave you clamoring for more after the last page is read."

—Love Romances and More

A Shared Range

"This is one of those stories to read when your heart is bruised and your world feels dark. You'll take a deep breath afterwards and see the sun again."

—Long and Short Reviews (Whipped Cream Reviews)

"…another enjoyable read filled with two well rounded and likable guys in Dakota and Wally, a great premise, a beautifully described mountain locale and two fun and interesting supporting characters."

—Literary Nymphs

http://www.dreamspinnerpress.com

To service members everywhere for the freedoms you protect and defend, including my freedom to write what I do.

Chapter One

THE short Wyoming range grass poked at his chest as he belly-crawled in the direction of the house. He ignored the pricks, scratches, and jabs as he kept his mind and attention on his objective—a cluster of cages behind the house. He really didn't care why he'd been contracted to infiltrate this particular ranch or why he'd been told specifically to get unseen to those cages and release the abused and malnourished animals inside. Gordon wiped his brow and kept moving. The lights had gone out in the house a while ago, darkness and near silence descending quickly on the land. Once his eyes adjusted to the dark, Gordon had been pleased he'd checked things out earlier in the day. If there was one thing he could count on, it was an innate sense of direction. It didn't matter if he couldn't see a thing anymore after he'd spotted a point or landmark—he could make a beeline to it and usually put himself over it with no difficulty at all.

Some light from the area around the barn combined with the partial moon to provide more than Gordon actually needed, and the cages loomed easily within his line of sight. Raising his body off the ground, he thought about getting up and walking from here, but his instructions had been very specific: he was not to be seen under any circumstances. And if at all possible, Gordon was to make every effort to make it look like someone had left the cages open and the poor, mistreated animals had gotten loose. He was pretty sure that the people who'd contacted him were some sort of ecoterrorist group or something like that. What Gordon really cared about was that they had paid him in cash, and he desperately needed the money because he hated starving.

A sound behind him had Gordon stopping where he was. Dropping to his belly again, he listened and waited, but heard nothing more. Looking around as best he could, he saw no one, and was pretty sure there wasn't any movement. Slowly, he began moving again. The cool night air had started to make its way through his clothing, and he wished he'd worn another layer, but it was too late now. He was getting close to the cages. He heard another sound and figured it was small creatures moving through the grass, and if he didn't keep moving, he'd have them to contend with as well, so Gordon moved closer and closer to the first set of cages. At the edge of the enclosures, he settled again and listened. Gordon could hear animals moving around in the cages. They didn't make a great deal of noise, but when he carefully lifted his head to look, he could see dark forms moving around. "Don't worry, you'll be free soon," Gordon whispered, sending the animals his best wishes as he got even closer.

Thinking he could use the cages themselves as cover, Gordon shifted direction and began moving behind them and around to the far side. That was when he ran into trouble. Gordon was approaching the cage on the farthest side when he heard a snarl that nearly curdled his blood. He tried to move away but realized he was too close to the cage, and a pair of razor claws raked over his leg. Stealth or not, money or not, Gordon let out a yell that reverberated over the land and echoed off the hills at the edge of the valley. Lights came on from every direction. Gordon rolled away from the cage and kept rolling, getting farther and farther away. His leg hurt like flaming hell. He was scared to touch it, but he knew he was bleeding and his pants were now wet and clinging to him—that is, what was left of his pants.

Voices called from around him, and Gordon kept putting distance between himself and the sounds. He decided to settle in the grass and wait until everyone left before getting the hell out of here. "Are all the animals okay?" Gordon heard what sounded like a concerned voice ask as figures walked from cage to cage, everyone keeping away from the cage he'd gone near.

"Yes, they're fine," a man answered, shining a flashlight around the cages and on the animals inside. Gordon stopped breathing when he realized that the cage he'd gotten close to contained a tiger. Holy shit! There were lions and black prowling cats in the other cages. Fuck, if he'd actually opened one of the cages, he'd probably have been ripped to shreds. Putting his head on the ground, Gordon wondered how in hell he got himself into messes like this all the time. Well, not necessarily like this, because this was the first time he'd actually come close to being torn apart by wild animals. Before he'd only been shot at, not ripped apart and eaten. They'd told him the cages contained exotic animals, and he'd been expecting zebras and animals like the ones he used to visit at the petting zoo when he was a kid.

Gordon tried to breathe and wait out the activity happening closer to the house. It was still dark enough that the people around the cages couldn't see him, but he had no intention of moving until they were gone. Then he was going to somehow make his way back to his pathetic excuse for a car and get the hell out of this town and, if he lived that long, the entire state.

The activity calmed down, and one by one, the people went inside. Once he couldn't see anyone else, Gordon got to his knees, gritting his teeth as he crawled farther and farther back across the field.

"I suggest if you want to continue breathing that you don't move another muscle," a gruff voice said, and Gordon stopped and slowly lifted his gaze. He saw what looked like a pair of boots and then sturdy legs, followed by a wide body and big arms holding a gun. Not knowing what else to do, Gordon put his head back down and waited to see what was going to happen next. "Are you injured?"

"Yes," Gordon answered honestly. He'd been caught and was being held at gunpoint. Honesty was his only way out now, if there was a way out of this. The people who'd hired him had told him that the owners of this ranch were ruthless animal abusers and that there was no telling what they'd do to him if he were to get caught. The worst had happened, and while Gordon thought about getting up and trying to make a run for it, his leg hurt so badly now, he wasn't sure he'd be able walk, let alone run.

"Okay. Here's what we're going to do. I'm going to take you to my place and have a look at your leg. I'll have my gun and I know damned well how to use it. In return for not shooting, you are going to tell me what in hell you were doing out in the range in the middle of the night and what on earth possessed you to get within a mile of that cage. That tiger would have ripped you to pieces in seconds."

Gordon nodded and the man lifted him up and onto his feet. His leg throbbed, but he was able to put a small amount of weight on it.

"Wally, it's Mario. I caught the guy who was out by the cages. That bitch of yours nailed him good on the leg. I'm bringing him to my place. You might want to see if Dakota can stop by and take a look. He's lost some blood and he's probably going to need stitches and maybe someone to examine his head." Gordon saw the other man looking at him as he talked on his cell phone. "Okay, I'll see you there." He hung up. "Can you walk?"

"A little, I guess," Gordon said. "I'm not armed." He'd been shot at plenty over the years and somehow he'd always made it home.

"Okay, but one move I don't like and I'll drop you in a heap," Mario said, though Gordon was hurting too badly to put up any sort of fight. In the end, that was why he'd gotten sent home. He couldn't take the sound of the gunfire, bombs, and God knew what else, any longer. In the end, whenever anyone pointed a gun at him, his mind no longer tried to figure out how to kill them first to get out of the situation. He simply dropped to the ground and hoped whoever had the gun wouldn't shoot him. The military didn't need men like that, so they'd discharged him medically and sent him home.

Slowly, Gordon and his helper made it toward a small building on the edge of the ranch. It wasn't too far from where he'd been caught, thank God, because Gordon wasn't sure how much longer his leg was going to hold out.

The inside of the cabin looked rather depressing, but the place was clean. Mario helped Gordon into a chair. "Don't move," Mario told him, and Gordon nodded. He wasn't sure he could even if he wanted to. For the first time he got a look at his shredded pant leg and the blood on the fabric. At least it didn't look too bad. He tried to move it, but pain shot up and down his leg, so he gave up. The next time he went anywhere, it was probably going to be a one-way ride to jail.

Mario returned with a pan of water as the door opened and two other men came in. One was large and carried a bag, while the other was smaller, but with huge eyes. "I'm Dakota Holden, and you're on my ranch. Who the hell are you?" the larger man said.

"Gordon Fisher," he answered.

"Lucky for you, I also happen to be a doctor. I'm going to take a look at your leg, since cat scratches can be incredibly infectious. Once I'm done, you're going to explain what you thought you were doing out by the cat cages."

Gordon nodded, and Dakota knelt on the floor. Fabric tore as Dakota ripped his pants up to his knee. "How bad is it?" Gordon asked.

"You're very lucky. The tiger didn't get a good purchase on your leg or else the rips in your flesh would be a lot deeper. Her claws are designed to rip flesh from bone. She didn't get the chance with you, but she won't fail the next time."

Gordon hissed between his teeth as Dakota cleaned his skin.

"What were you doing out there?" the third man asked.

"I was hired to set them all free," Gordon explained, and the smaller man gasped. "What? They're in little cages."

The man stalked in front of Gordon. "Those animals are rescues from circuses and carnivals. I take care of them, nurse them back to health in some cases, and then I find them good homes in zoos and other reputable places. Some of those cats have been with me for five years, and I have no idea what they would do outside those cages. I'm a veterinarian, for God's sake. I'd never hurt any animal in my care, but I may hurt you." The man's eyes blazed. "You're damned lucky you didn't let any of those cats loose. They would stalk any prey that came across their line of sight, and the first bit of prey would have been you. They'd have ripped you apart before moving on to scare half the community, until someone shot them."

"I didn't know. I was told you were hurting them and keeping them under bad conditions," Gordon whined slightly.

"Who in hell told you all that crap?" the man yelled. At the same time, Dakota pressed a cold cloth to part of his leg, and Gordon jumped.

"Those animals need my help to survive, and whoever told you they were being mistreated was full of crap!" The small man was still yelling, and Gordon's eyes widened. "I ought to show you pictures of the damaged feet and loss of hair I saw when they came in, and how good they look now."

"Wally, calm down," Dakota said without looking up from Gordon's leg.

"But the one attacked me," Gordon said, thankful he never got the cage open. Who knew what would have happened.

"She was beaten and whipped by her captors. They turned her into a cat that hates every human on the planet. If you'd let her go, she would have attacked you and then moved on to whoever else she found. Maybe the kid from the ranch down the road would have been next. Believe it or not, she's much better now. When Jasmine first got here, she spent her days banging against the cage, trying to get out. Now at least Liam and I can get close enough to feed her and take care of her without being attacked. But your little stunt has probably undone all that work!" Wally flashed him a look of total disgust and then whirled away from him. "When you're done, Kota, I want him off our ranch, and I don't care if he has to fucking crawl." Wally spun around and stalked out, and Gordon jumped when the door slammed hard enough to shake the walls.

Gordon looked down at the doctor treating his leg and heard him snickering. "You must have some sort of talent, because you managed to rile him up more than anyone has in years," Dakota said with an odd twinkle in his eyes.

"He sure talks big," Gordon said as the doctor got some bandages out of his bag.

Both Dakota and Mario started chuckling, which turned into full-on laughter. "That man may talk tough, but he can also kick your ass into the middle of next week," Mario told him. "He's one man you want to stay on the good side of."

"Were you in the service?" Dakota asked, and Gordon nodded. "You have the look." Dakota returned to his work. "When you went through basic, you had those guys you knew would always have your back no matter what, right?"

"Yeah," Gordon answered, remembering Stacks and Bottles, his best friends, both gone now.

"Well, that's the way Wally is. If he's your friend, he'll move heaven and earth for you, but piss him off or hurt someone he cares for, and even those lions and tigers out back wouldn't stand a chance. He knows how to fight and knows how to win, so you'd best not judge him by his size." Dakota stood up. "Besides, if you mess with my Wally, you mess with me too."

Gordon swallowed and nodded. "Thank you for your help."

Dakota nodded and put his things away before pulling over one of the kitchen chairs. "Now you're going to tell me who put you up to the stupid notion of trying to infiltrate my ranch." Gordon nodded, looking down at his leg and slowly rolling it so he could see the bandage. The claw marks extended out from under the gauze. "You were very lucky, and whoever put you up to this didn't know what the hell they were doing or what they were talking about."

Gordon nodded again and looked up at the other two men, who both sat straight and tall, staring at him intently. "I met them at a diner outside of town. They were looking for someone to help them with a problem, and I overheard their conversation. When I showed some interest, they pounced enthusiastically. Told me that some animals were being abused on this ranch and used for God knows what. They said they were being kept in tiny cages without enough food, water, or shelter. They wanted someone to let them free and were willing to pay."

"You know that was a bunch of crap," Dakota said, and Gordon nodded automatically. He didn't really know who to believe any longer, but the fact that the people who'd hired him to set the animals free didn't tell him that they were big cats that would rip him apart wasn't adding to their credibility. "Wally would give his life before he'd harm any creature." Gordon nodded again. "What did these people look like?"

At least now he could provide information. "There were four of them, three men and a woman. I met them yesterday. All were in their midtwenties and looked a bit like hippies. The leader called himself Rafe. Tall, about six feet, with dirty-blond hair and blue eyes that never seemed to settle anywhere. The woman was probably his girlfriend. She didn't say much. Short dark hair, wild eyes, nose that had probably been broken at least once. Figured someone used her for a punching bag at one time. No bruises now, though." Once Gordon started, the words poured out. He didn't owe those people any loyalty, and at least Dakota and Mario had helped him. "The other two were twins, both middle height, brown hair, goatees. Looked like a matched set."

"Anything else you can tell us? Did they say where they were heading?" Dakota asked, and Gordon shook his head.

"No. They sounded like they were staying put for a while. Like this area needed to be cleaned out or something," Gordon explained, thinking back on the conversation they'd had in the diner the day before. "They wanted me to join their group, and I think this was some sort of initiation."

"Why did you agree to do this?" Mario asked, clearly confused.

"I like helping animals. They don't shoot at me," Gordon answered truthfully, and both men looked at each other and nodded slightly.

"I'm going to pass this information to the sheriff. If he catches them, we'll need you to identify them. If you help us, I won't press charges against you," Dakota said as he stood up, stifling a yawn. "I want to check your leg in the morning to make sure there's no infection."

"Okay," Gordon answered, not sure what was going to happen next. Dakota walked over to where Mario stood and the two of them talked softly. Mario nodded a few times and flicked his gaze in Gordon's direction, but he couldn't hear what either of them said. Then Dakota left, and Mario disappeared down what must have been a small hallway before returning with a blanket, a pillow, and a pair of jeans for Gordon to wear in the morning.

"You can sleep on the sofa," Mario commanded and passed him the bedding. "Don't go wandering through the house and don't think of leaving. I hear everything, and the sheriff will probably want to talk to you in the morning."

"I won't go anywhere," Gordon promised. He didn't have a place to go unless he wanted to sleep in his car again, and that prospect wasn't something he was looking forward to.

Mario nodded and left the room, turning out the lights as he went. Gordon stretched out on the sofa, getting as comfortable as he could before turning out the light near his head. His leg ached and he knew it probably would all night long. Gordon managed to find a reasonably comfortable position and closed his eyes. At least he was warm and springs weren't jabbing into his back. In the morning, he'd do what they wanted and try to keep his ass out of jail. Then he'd take off and get out of these people's hair. He remembered his mother saying years ago that they had relatives up in Montana. Maybe he'd try to look them up to see if one of them could help him get a job.

Chapter Two

MARIO didn't sleep much. He wasn't used to having someone else in the house with him, and every sound reminded him of David. More than once, he rolled over expecting to feel David sleeping in the bed next to him, but of course it was empty. It had been just shy of two years, and David wasn't coming back. They'd had a good life together while it lasted, but their relationship had cooled off toward the end, and eventually David had moved on. Mario couldn't really blame him. For the last year, they'd been together but not really together. It was hard to put into words, but the best way to explain it was that they'd grown apart. Still, it didn't matter, with his mind playing tricks on him and every sound in the house raising ghosts. Mario checked the clock and groaned. He didn't have to get up for another hour and he was damned well tired enough to sleep. Dang dreams. Mario rolled over before punching his pillow a few times, trying to get some sleep. But every time he closed his eyes, he heard the other man, the man with the lost puppy eyes, shifting on the living room sofa.

Mario got out of bed and went to the bathroom, splashing water on his face before going back to bed. He must have fallen asleep because he woke with a start to rapping on his door.

"Hey, old man, it's time to get going," Dakota said through the door, and Mario groaned as he got out of bed. After pulling on a pair of jeans, he opened the bedroom door before searching for a clean shirt. He shrugged on the first one he found before turning to face his boss. "You look like hell," Dakota told him.

"Thanks. I love you too," Mario retorted as he sat on the edge of the bed, pulling on his socks and then his boots. Dakota had way too much energy in the damned mornings. Mario used to be like that as well, but that seemed to be history. Mario finished dressing and followed Dakota down the hall. "Where's our guest?" he asked when he saw the neatly folded blanket, the pillow resting on top of it, but no Gordon.

"Last I saw, he was out by the main paddock watching the horses. Couldn't seem to take his eyes off them," Dakota said. He handed Mario the travel mug from off the table, and Mario tipped it back, hot coffee sliding down his throat like the nectar of the gods.

"Is he out there alone?" Mario asked, picking up the pace before Gordon could do more damage.

"No. He's with the hands, and I don't think he's gonna try anything. He's just watching the horses do their thing. I read about cases like him when I was in med school. Some guys, when they come home, relive the war in their minds again and again, while others run the opposite way, become as docile as house cats, and wouldn't hurt a fly. I think that's the kind we've got out there."

Mario shook his head like Dakota had gone crazy. "Kind of what?"

"Veteran," Dakota said. "I'm willing to bet Gordon was in Iraq or Afghanistan and that he probably saw more than his fair share of combat. His way of dealing with it is to retreat from anything confrontational. He loves animals because they don't shoot at him. I'm willing to bet Gordon has had plenty of people shooting at him at one time or other."

"Jesus," Mario groaned as he followed Dakota toward the barn, sipping more coffee as he went. Sure enough, he saw Gordon leaning on the paddock fence while one of the hands worked with the chestnut mare Dakota had bought a few weeks back. Gordon didn't look up and barely seemed to notice as Mario walked up to him.

"Nice horse," Gordon said eventually. "But she's got a problem with her hind leg you should have the vet look at." Gordon didn't even look away from where the horse was trotting. Mario watched and didn't see a thing other than a good healthy stride and plenty of energy. He continued watching.

"Kyle, get Wally," he told the kid exercising the mare. "I want him to take a look at her." Mario didn't see anything wrong, but maybe he'd missed something. Kyle hurried out of the paddock, closing the gate behind him before rushing to the house. A few minutes later, he came back out with Wally right behind him.

Wally walked over to where they were standing, and Mario saw Wally glare at Gordon for a moment and then turn to him. "What is it you want me to see?"

"Would you check the mare's hind leg?" Mario asked. Wally looked at him like he was crazy, but entered the paddock and ran his hands up and down the horse's legs, stopping at the leg Gordon had indicated.

"It's warm," Wally said with a bit of surprise. "How did you know?" he asked Mario, who shrugged and looked at Gordon. Wally repeated the question.

Gordon shrugged. "She just walked different on that leg sometimes," Gordon said softly.

"Take her into the barn and let her rest. I need to check her further," Wally told Kyle, who nodded and slowly led the horse away. "You really saw something was wrong?" Wally asked Gordon.

"Didn't know what it was, but she was pained every now and then. Took me a few minutes to isolate the leg as the cause. Is she going to be okay?" Gordon asked, and Wally nodded. "Good. She's a beautiful horse."

"That she is, and she'll be fine." Wally turned to Mario. "The sheriff should be here soon. Watch out for him, and then he and Gordon need to talk." Wally hurried into the barn.

"Where do you live?" Mario asked Gordon as he finished the last of his coffee.

"Here and there. Don't rightly have a permanent home or nothing," Gordon said. Any further conversation was cut off by one of the sheriff's vehicles pulling into the drive. They waited for him to pull to a stop and get out of the car. Gordon introduced himself, and then he and the sheriff stepped away. Mario let them talk and went to work, doling out the day's assignments and making sure all the chores that needed done were getting done. The sheriff and Gordon finished pretty quickly, and the sheriff went off in search of Dakota.

"I take it you have a car someplace?" Mario asked, and Gordon nodded. "I can take you to it if you want, and you can get on home. Dakota said he wasn't pressing charges." Gordon nodded again, and Mario walked to his truck and waited for Gordon to get in. Then he started the engine and pulled down the driveway, the old thing bouncing as they went. Once they were on the street, the ride smoothed out.

"It's on the side road," Gordon said, and Mario turned, heading along the side of the ranch. Sure enough, they came on a blue sedan that had definitely seen better days. Mario pulled off behind it and got out while Gordon did the same. "Thanks for not sending me to jail. I'm sorry for any trouble I caused. I'll be heading out and won't darken your doorstep again."

Mario didn't know quite what to say as Gordon pulled open the driver's door. Mario walked alongside the car and saw blankets in the backseat along with packs of food on the floor. "Have you been living out of this?" Mario asked, and Gordon looked up from the driver's seat, nodding slowly with as much dignity as he seemed able to muster. "How long have you been living out of your car?" Gordon shrugged and didn't say anything. "Follow me back to the ranch," Mario said, trying to think quickly of a reason. "Dakota still needs to take a look at those scratches."

Gordon looked skeptical, but started the engine, and Mario got back in his truck and led the way back to the ranch. When they pulled in, Mario saw Wally poke his head out of the barn, throwing him a momentary look that would turn most people to stone if it were possible. Mario parked and got out. "Dakota wanted to check his scratches for infection before he left," Mario said lamely, but he knew Wally wasn't buying it. Thankfully, Dakota heard the exchange and led Gordon into the house.

"Why'd you bring him back?" Wally hissed.

"He's living out of his car," Mario said and instantly Wally's expression softened. "He's been doing it for some time by the looks of things. No wonder it was so easy for those eco types to talk him into that crap last night. The guy's probably pretty desperate for money." Mario wandered over to the sedan and gazed through the windows. "A few blankets, a dinky cooler, a bag of canned goods, and whatever's in the trunk," he said out loud for Wally's benefit. "He did help us with that mare today."

"Are you saying we should let him stay here after what he did?" Wally asked.

"You're going to turn him out?" Mario pressed, already knowing the answer. Wally could talk big sometimes, but the guy had a heart of gold and there was no way he was going to turn away some guy who'd been living in his car, probably for months. "We do need a hand to help in the barn," Mario reminded him.

Wally shook his head slowly. "You know Dakota and I don't interfere with how you and Haven run the ranch. If he's okay with hiring him, then so are we. But he's your responsibility, and have you thought where he's going to live?" Wally asked with mischief in his eyes. "I thought so." Wally grinned as he walked toward the house, and a few minutes later Gordon came out and headed for his car.

Mario stopped Gordon as he headed for his car. "Look, I need someone to help in the barn, and I was wondering if you could use some work?" God, he was so going to regret this.

"You're offering me a job?" Gordon asked, obviously not believing what Mario had told him. "After what I've done?" Gordon shook his head. "You're just joking with me." He continued heading to his car, and Mario followed.

"I'm not joking," Mario said. Gordon stopped, whirling around.

"Why? You don't know crap about me except that I tried to break onto your property. Why would you ever offer me a job?" Gordon didn't wait for an answer, and Mario felt a tinge of panic rise in his gut. He had no idea why Gordon staying was suddenly so very important, but it was. He should simply let him go and hire someone else to work in the barn. Hell, he didn't even know if Gordon knew the first thing about horses other than their walk changes when they're hurting.

"Gordon," Mario said softly, using the same voice he used with a spooked horse, calm and low. "You were put up to what you did because you thought you were helping creatures in trouble. I believe that. I don't think you'd hurt anyone or anything," Mario added, and Gordon stopped with his hand on the car door handle.

"You don't know what I'm capable of," Gordon told him. "I've done things that…." The pained expression that flashed across Gordon's eyes for a split second went straight to Mario's heart. He saw Gordon's legs wobble beneath him, and on impulse, he reached out to Gordon. Mario took his arm, and when he didn't pull away, Mario led him across the yard to stand by one of the paddocks, figuring Gordon could use the fence for support.

"Do you want to talk about it?" Mario asked, not surprised in the least when Gordon shook his head.

"Were you really serious about the job?" Gordon asked, and Mario nodded. Their eyes met for a brief second, Gordon's brown puppy eyes giving Mario a glimpse of the pain and loss he carried deep inside.

"Yes, I was serious," Mario answered.

"But what about Wally? He can't be happy about me working here," Gordon asked.

"Don't worry about Wally," Mario said, and Gordon flashed him an extremely skeptical look. "He's a guy who takes in lions and tigers so he can help them. I've seen Wally sit with a sick horse for days. He's got the biggest heart of any person I've ever met."

Gordon stared at the horse happily eating the grass on the far side of the paddock. He said nothing for a long time and then slowly turned his head to look at Mario. "Why would you do this?"

Mario had been asking himself the same thing for the last few minutes. He could easily get hands for the ranch, ones without Gordon's apparent baggage. Mario opened his mouth to answer the question and then closed it again because he really didn't have an answer that wouldn't sound lame when spoken out loud. "Don't look a gift horse in the mouth," Mario said, dodging the question that made him decidedly uncomfortable. Gordon nodded again, and Mario took that as agreement.

"What is it you need me to do?" Gordon asked, and Mario pointed to Kyle.

"Kyle, Gordon is going to work in the barn. Can you get him started?"

"Sure," Kyle said, motioning for Gordon to follow him. Mario turned back to the horse he'd been watching, telling himself over and over that he wasn't going to watch Gordon walk toward the barn. Of course, that lasted about two seconds, and Mario turned his head, watching Gordon's backside move a bit stiffly in those tight jeans. After a few seconds, he forced himself to look away. He so wasn't going to go there.

"Ready to check fence?" Dakota asked eagerly from behind him. "Haven says he needs help in the north range, and I sure could use some time away from the office."

"Whenever you are," Mario answered. "Let me get the supplies loaded in the truck and we can go. Shawn will drive it out. Five minutes?" Dakota agreed, and Mario sprang into action, enlisting the help of some of the other guys to load fence-repair materials on the ATVs. When Dakota was ready, they strapped on their helmets and took off across the land. The wind whipped around him as he bounced across the range toward the area he and Dakota were going to check. It had been quite a while since he and Dakota had worked together on any sort of project, and he'd missed spending time with his friend. He and Dakota had known each other for years. They raced each other, and Mario found himself smiling, truly smiling, for the first time in a while.

As they reached their destination, they slowed, and Dakota pulled up near the fence. "Need help unloading?" he asked as Shawn placed the repair materials where Mario had asked.

"Nah, this is the last of it. You two have fun," Shawn said, wiping his brow with the back of his gloved hand before heading back toward the truck.

"Thanks," Mario called, and Shawn lifted a hand in a quick wave before heading back to the house in a cloud of dust. "That way?" Mario pointed east, and Dakota nodded. They loaded the supplies they could carry on the ATVs and slowly began moving down the fence. This was usually lonely work, but they stuck together, since two sets of eyes were better than one.

"Is it just me, or has the ranch seemed…," Mario began but his voice trailed off.

"I know what you mean," Dakota said. "Since Dad's death, some of the spark has gone out of the place. It's been almost two years, and everyone is doing what they're supposed to, but it's like part of the place died when he did. And I don't know what to do to fix it." Dakota stopped. "I know it's been more than that for you." Mario nodded slowly, keeping his gaze on the fencing. "Have you heard from David at all?"

"A few times. He seems to have moved on pretty well. Last I heard, he was in Montana working a large spread. Seemed happy, but we didn't talk about anything important." Mario talked fast because speaking about David still hurt even after all this time. "We don't anymore." Mario stopped his ATV and got off, checking a weak-looking section of fence before signaling Dakota, who joined him. "We better strengthen this or we'll have a break soon, for sure."

Dakota agreed, and they got to work. Mario clipped away the rusting wire and Dakota began stringing the new. They fastened it to the posts and checked that they were sturdy before finishing up. "You know, it's okay to move on," Dakota said, and Mario nodded.

"Haven't found anyone to move on with," Mario replied, but he knew that wasn't exactly true. He'd had a few offers since David had left, but he hadn't been interested. "And I could say the same thing about you."

Dakota turned to him, and for a second Mario thought Dakota was going to blow up at him. He dropped his tools in the grass and placed his hands on his hips, staring at Mario. "You're right. It's time we all got past this thing with my dad. Next month we're having the summer barbeque the way we always used to, and it's going to be one hell of a party. It's time we all moved on." Dakota zeroed his gaze on him. "And that means you too." Mario rolled his eyes.

"I honestly thought David was the guy I was going to be with for the long haul, you know," Mario finally said as he inspected the repair and began packing up the supplies again. Dakota gathered up the old wire and carefully rolled it up. "Never thought that before him, and maybe I'm not meant to be like that with anyone." Mario closed the latch on the small cargo hatch and climbed on the ATV. He started the engine and moved slowly down the fence line. Dakota followed, and Mario kept his mind on the task at hand, no matter how many times it threatened to wander to thoughts of Gordon. Why that kept happening he didn't know, but he was somehow going to put a stop to it. He didn't need that kind of heartache again.

He and Dakota worked the rest of the morning. They repaired a few other areas of fence before gathering the last of the supplies and heading back toward the house. Mario had been keeping an eye on clouds massing on the western horizon. They'd slowly built and gotten closer through the course of the morning and early afternoon. He wasn't about to complain about some rain, but there was a lot of work to get done, and it would be great if the rain could hold off until nightfall, but it didn't look like that was in the cards. "We better hurry," Dakota called, and they both sped up, racing as the wind came up, bringing the darker clouds with it.

They pulled into the equipment garage and then joined the others. Dakota led horses into the barn, Gordon closed and locked gates behind him, and Mario had anything loose carried inside or battened down. "Gordon," Mario said as he hurried out of the garage, "have you seen Wally?"

"No," he answered.

"Come on," Mario said as he headed around the side of the ranch house. Mario headed out to the cages, where the cats were all prowling like the nervously caged beasts they were. "Stay back and man that gate," Mario explained as he pointed toward the slide to close the cage. "We need to get this big boy into his own cage, where he can hunker down." He clanged on the back of the cage, and the large cat prowled toward the sound. "Close it," Mario cried, and Gordon shut the gate, securing the lion in his home. "They'll be fine, but in a storm like this, if they have too much room, they might be able to get up enough speed to hurt themselves."

"Thanks, guys," Wally said as he hurried up with Liam, his assistant, right behind him. "These guys will be fine, but—" Wally pointed to the other grouping of cages a short distance away. "We need to get them secured as well and we don't have much time." The wind picked up, and Liam was already hurrying toward the cages, carrying a metal tray. Liam lured the panther from the common area into his cage with some meat, and Gordon closed the gate like he had done previously. Wally hurried, dropping food in each cage. "They'll be calmer if they've eaten."

The first drops of rain appeared on the wind. Mario helped inspect all the cages, and then the men hurried back to the first grouping, Wally and Liam dropping meat into each cage as they went. Then they all hurried toward the back door of the house as the rain came in huge drops. Liam pulled the door open, and seconds after the sky opened up, they dashed inside.

None of them appeared too wet, but Wally got towels for all of them, and they dried off as best they could. Mario watched the rain come down in sheets and began making a list in his head of all the things they would need to check for damage once this was over. Granted, rain of any type was generally a blessing this time of year, but this much rain this fast could also cause washouts and minor flooding, especially along the smaller streams and creeks. "You really take good care of them," Gordon said to Wally, nodding in the direction of the cages.

"Of course we do," Liam said indignantly and walked away. He returned to where they were sort of drip-drying and shoved a picture into Gordon's hand. "That's Wally and Schian," Liam said. Mario knew the picture but leaned over Gordon's shoulder anyway. The huge lion lay on his back, paws in the air, while Wally rubbed his belly.

"He was the first big cat I rescued, and he's the only one I trusted enough to get that close to," Wally explained. "Schian was old and I didn't have him that long, but he acted like a big housecat and loved to be scratched. You could hear him purr halfway across the ranch when he got going." Mario saw Dakota join them, gathering Wally into his arms. "Shahrazad was the meanest cat I ever had. That bitch would as soon take your arm off as look at you." Wally gazed up at Dakota. "She's a Bengal, and once she settled down, I was able to find a place to take her. She's now the star attraction at a zoo in the Northeast, lives in tigerly bliss, and has even had a few cubs. I get pictures of her from her keepers every now and then."

"No animal on this ranch has ever been abused or neglected," Mario said.

Gordon nodded slowly and said nothing more.

The rain tapered off. A short while later, the sun came back out, raising the heat and humidity level to somewhere near broiling. Everyone spent the rest of the day cleaning up from the storm and finishing up the list of chores that never seemed to go down, as far as Mario was concerned, anyway. He didn't see Gordon for the rest of the day, but once Wally called and invited both him and Gordon for dinner up at the house, the fluttery nerves started up again. What was it about Gordon that got under his skin?

Chores done, most of the guys heading out for the night, Mario walked into the main house to find Liam and Troy, Liam's partner, along with Gordon, sitting around the table while Wally worked in the kitchen. Dakota joined them a few minutes later. "I have to go into town. I have an emergency call at the hospital," he explained before leaning toward Wally, kissing him lightly. "I'll be back as soon as I can."

Wally took it in stride. They both had hectic schedules, but in all the years he'd known them, Mario had never seen them stay angry with each other for more than a few minutes. And even when they fought, they still seemed to support one another. He wanted that kind of relationship, one built on a foundation so deep and loving that nothing could shake it. He'd thought he had that with David, but he'd definitely been wrong. "Go ahead and take a seat," Wally said as he carried dishes to the table, then returned with plates and silverware. "Don't stand on ceremony," he continued as he brought still more food.

Gordon got up and followed Wally, returning with a dish of salad that he set on the table. Everyone took a place, and Mario found himself sitting next to Gordon. He turned to Mario and smiled a little. Gordon was cute in a big-guy way. Maybe it was the baby face. Mario wasn't sure, but he warmed slightly at the smile.

"So, Gordon, were you in the service?" Liam asked as he passed the salad.

"I was a Marine," Gordon said quietly, and Mario noticed he refused to meet anyone's gaze.

"Were you in the wars?" Liam continued.

"I fought in both Iraq and Afghanistan," Gordon said. "And before you ask, it wasn't what you saw on television. It was ten times worse than anything you could possibly imagine."

Mario saw Gordon's hand shake slightly when he took the bowl. "Did all the cats make it through the storm?" Mario asked to change the subject.

"Yes. They're as happy as can be. This weather reminds most of them of home, and the last I looked, most of them were lying in the shade, taking a snooze," Wally answered with a slight nod that told Mario he'd clearly picked up on the change of subject. "I'd like to build a third enclosure this week," Wally said as he looked at Mario. "Do you think we can work that into the schedule? I'll need some manpower for a day or two and I've already put together the schematic and list of building supplies we'll need." He pulled a piece of paper out of his shirt pocket and handed it to Mario. "If it doesn't rain, we can pour the concrete footings once we get the foundations dug."

"Foundations?" Gordon asked, lifting his gaze from his plate.

"Cats can dig, so I pour a concrete foundation and barrier around the edge of each cage, deep enough that they can't dig under it. We set the posts in the concrete and then build the enclosures. I don't want the cats spending their days on concrete, but I don't want them loose, either. This way each one gets natural grass to live on while ensuring they stay where they're supposed to."

"I'll get the supplies ordered," Mario said as he placed the list in his pocket. "And if the weather holds and the herd stays where they're supposed to, we should be able to get to it this week or early next week."

"That's fine. But I must have them in less than two weeks. There's a circus passing through, and they've already contacted me about taking a few of their cats. They're getting old and need a proper home. So we need to have one ready for them."

"Do you advertise?" Gordon asked, and Wally shook his head. "Then how do they know about you?"

"I work with circuses all the time. Word gets around that I'll take their older animals. They don't want to hurt them, but can't afford to keep an animal that's too old to work. I don't care how old they are, I'll do my best to give them the best retirement possible. That's how I got Schian." Wally ate, and Mario glanced at Gordon. "He was my first and the one I was closest to. It was hard when he died, but all the cats, docile or the biggest cat bitch alive, are special to me, and they all deserve to live as happy and contented a life as possible." Wally seemed to realize he'd gotten a bit on his high horse and turned his attention to his plate.

"I'll help you build your enclosures. It's the least I can do," Gordon said before returning to his dinner. It seemed Wally had won Gordon over, and without thinking about it, Mario lightly bumped Gordon's shoulder, and he bumped him back in some unspoken message of pleased solidarity.

The meal continued with plenty of talk about the ranch and the prospects for the year. Once they were done, everyone helped clear the table. Phillip and Haven came in as Wally brought ice cream and toppings to the table. Of course, they joined them, as did Dakota once he returned. By the time he pushed back from the table, Mario was stuffed to the gills. He leaned back in his chair and breathed deeply, letting the food digest slightly, his eyes automatically drifting closed in total contentment.

"Where do I stay?" Gordon whispered to Mario softly as the others continued eating. That was one thing about ranch work—everyone worked up one hell of an appetite. Mario peered at Gordon and clearly saw he expected to be told to sleep in his car. Of course, that wasn't going to happen.

"With me," Mario answered before he could second-guess the offer. "You can stay on the sofa tonight, and tomorrow we'll see about clearing out the extra bedroom." He and David had used that room for storage for years and he'd never got around to cleaning it out. He'd sort of closed the door and tried to forget about what was in there. "Thanks for everything, Wally, it was a great meal, but I need to hit the hay so I can be up early in the morning." Mario got up, and after a few good-nights, he left the room. Gordon said his thank-yous and good-nights as well.

Together they walked across the yard to the foreman's house, stopping at Gordon's car for some of his things, and once inside, Mario stared at the sofa with his small pile of bedding for a few minutes, feeling a bit guilty and wondering how he could give Gordon a more comfortable place to sleep.

"Don't worry about it," Gordon said. "I slept in the car for two weeks before last night. The sofa is comfortable enough."

"We have a hard day tomorrow," Mario said as Gordon began spreading out the bedding.

"I'll pull my weight," Gordon told him with a touch of pride.

"I didn't doubt that. I...," Mario began, but the words stopped in his throat as Gordon turned away from him and pulled off his shirt. He'd known Gordon was strong, but seeing his wide shoulders tapering to a small waist, pale skin glistening with just a hint of sweat, part of Mario wanted Gordon to turn around so he could see the chest and arms that went with that back. But the rest of him didn't want Gordon to see him staring like a lovesick teenager. Mario swallowed hard to help make his voice work. "The bathroom is down the hall if you'd like to clean up. I'll set out towels and stuff for you." Mario forced himself to turn away. "I'll see you in the morning." With almost alarming speed, Mario hurried to his room. Gathering his things, he listened for movement, but heard nothing, so he hurried to the bathroom and took a quick shower, forcing himself not to think about Gordon out in the other room. Once he was done, he went back to his room, and after he closed his door, he heard Gordon moving around and then a few minutes later, he heard the shower start.

Mario got in bed and rolled onto his side, punching his pillow and trying to get comfortable and to keep the thoughts he shouldn't be having about one of the hands out of his mind. Finally, the water turned off and he once again heard Gordon moving around. Mario allowed himself a few minutes of fantasy as he wondered what Gordon looked like padding down the hallway to the living room. Was he wearing his underwear or maybe just a towel round his narrow waist? Rolling over once again, he struggled to get comfortable and to push the lascivious thoughts from his head. A soft grunt reached his ears, followed by the squeak of the sofa and then nothing. The house quieted completely, and Mario closed his eyes, quickly falling into a deep sleep.

A scream split the night, and Mario jumped out of bed. His clock flashed 3:30. Opening his bedroom door, Mario listened, but the house was quiet. Mario closed the door again and pushed open his window, listening for any sounds that shouldn't be there. But everything was exactly the way it should be—crickets chirped, horses neighed and moved in their paddocks, and the occasional lowing of cattle whispered in on the breeze. Mario wondered if he'd imagined the whole thing and climbed back into bed. He closed his eyes and was half-asleep when another scream rent the night, this one louder and more horrifying than the first.

Mario's feet barely touched the floor as he hurried out of the room and down the hall. Gordon tossed on the sofa for a few minutes and then seemed to settle, his eyes still closed. Mario thought about waking him, but didn't know how he'd react. Gordon's tossing quieted further, and he rolled over, the sofa squeaking as he did. Not knowing what else to do, Mario left him and went back to his room, closing the door behind him and hoping the rest of the night would be quiet.

Chapter Three

THE heat from the blinding sun seared its way through everything—Gordon's clothes and even his skin, all the way to his bones. And the sand—in everything and places where sand was not meant to be felt, not now, not ever. He and the rest of his unit were on patrol, Stacks on one side and Bottles on the other, like they had been for years. Gordon could see the house they were to take in the distance. Sweat poured down his back, but he ignored it as they got closer and closer to what they'd been told was an abandoned building with a vantage point the rest of the unit needed. They got nearer and were almost there when all hell broke loose. Rockets shot overheard, bullets struck the ground all around them, and Gordon hit the deck like he'd been trained before trying to assess where the fire was coming from. It wasn't from the house, but off to the side. *"Marines get scared, but they're still the ones running toward the bullets."* That was what they'd been told, so that was what they did. The gunfire got louder, and the nerves in Gordon's stomach shook even as he moved closer. Men screamed around him, and then Gordon....

He woke with a thump staring up at the sofa from the floor, where he'd landed, the blankets tangled around his legs, his breath coming in shallow pants, heart racing. His mind took a few seconds to clear and he realized he wasn't in Fallujah, but on a ranch in Wyoming.

"Are you okay?"

Gordon saw Mario hurry into the room and turn on the light by the sofa.

"I heard you fall off the sofa." Mario touched his arm and helped him off the floor. Gordon was tempted to pull away, but the gentle touch on his skin felt nice. No one had touched him that way in a very long time, and he liked it. After getting his feet under him, Gordon stood as his gaze caught Mario's, and he saw the other man color slightly even as his eyes widened.

What surprised Gordon was the hurt and pain he saw deep inside Mario. He recognized them easily, but to see them reflected back at him from such an unexpected place nearly made Gordon collapse again. But he kept his balance and managed to sit back on the sofa. "Were you back there?" Mario asked softly, and Gordon nodded.

"I didn't mean to wake you. Sometimes the memories come forward when I don't want them to," Gordon said. "It happens to lots of guys."

"Have you gotten any help? I understand there are things they can do."

"There's not. Yeah, I talked to lots of headshrinkers, but there's nothing they can do. They wanted to put me on all kinds of drugs, but who wants to live their life through a haze of Percoshit and Darvocrap or whatever they gave me? I may lose sleep sometimes, but at least what I got is all me." Gordon touched his head and saw Mario smile. "I'm sorry if I woke you."

Mario shook his head. "Truth be told, I usually don't sleep very well." Gordon wasn't sure if Mario was telling him the truth or just trying to make him feel better. "I haven't slept well in quite a while."

"What's got you worked up?" Gordon asked as he settled back on the sofa. He thought he knew the answer, because for a few seconds he'd followed Mario's gaze as it seemed to rake over his bare skin. Most everyone on the ranch seemed to be gay, and Gordon had sort of figured Mario was too. He didn't mind.

"Nothing," Mario answered quickly and then looked away. "Will you tell me what it was really like over there?" He settled on the far side of the sofa. "You don't have to tell me anything painful, I just sort of want to understand."

Gordon got this question a lot from people he met, and he hated talking about it. "Heat, hotter than you can imagine. Sand everywhere. I never want to go to a beach for as long as I live. The thought of being in a bathing suit around that much sand ever again...." Gordon let the words hang as he shook his head. "You're surrounded by people and you don't know if they hate you, love you, or just don't give a damn as long as you aren't shooting at them." Gordon kept his voice level and his thoughts in the here and now. He knew it would be easy to close his eyes and then he'd be right back there, transported through time and distance, and all the crap he'd lived through would start over again.

"There had to be good times," Mario said softly, and Gordon gave in to the urge.

"There were. There was this place at the corner of one of the bases. It wasn't much, but it's where we used to gather to have a beer. There wasn't a real bar or anything, but it was sort of our spot. We all used to talk about home and the people we left behind. Most of the guys had wives, some had kids, a few had babies they'd never seen. One of my best friends, Stacks, he was as tall as they came and he had this tiny wife." Gordon snickered. "We all knew who was on top in that relationship." Gordon couldn't help smiling at the old joke. "We'd returned for another tour and a month later, his wife writes that she's three months pregnant and sends him a picture of the sonogram. Stacks yelled loud enough that half of Iraq could hear him. He got pictures of her while she was pregnant, and then when she had the baby, I'll never forget the first pictures she e-mailed him of his daughter. Pretty little thing."

"Did he get to see her?" Mario asked, and Gordon shook his head, looking down at the sofa cushions between them.

"I saw her and the baby when I got home. Wonderful lady, and the most beautiful daughter that he never got to see." Gordon yawned because he had to stop talking about this stuff. It was too painful.

"I know Marines are supposed to be strong and all, but it's okay to feel the loss of your friends. It doesn't make you less of a man." Mario stood up and walked closer to where Gordon sat. "If you want the truth, I think it makes you more of a man to let yourself feel what you feel." Mario lightly touched his shoulder, and Gordon stiffened for a second and then placed his hand on top of Mario's. It wasn't the feeling that he was afraid of, but what came afterward. The things he didn't want to think about or remember, let alone talk about with anyone.

"Thanks," Gordon said, because it was all he could get his lips to form. He yawned again, and slowly Mario pulled his hand away. "I better go back to sleep or I won't be worth anything in the morning." He had to say something. Gordon had worked on an hour of sleep for days and he could do it again, but he needed time alone, to think. Mario made him want things he didn't think he could have or should be able to have.

Mario nodded and turned away. Gordon watched Mario's backside retreat and then he lay back on the sofa and turned out the light. But sleep didn't come. He was almost afraid of it. Gordon didn't want to dream again, and he didn't want to keep Mario up with his disturbed dreams. After a while, his eyes sort of closed on their own, and he fell into a restless sleep. He didn't dream, thankfully, but he didn't really sleep either.

Gordon woke again to a quiet house. He got up, dressed, and folded his bedding like he had the day before and then headed outside. He was greeted like he had been the day before, by horses in their paddocks and near total quiet. Gordon watched them for a few minutes before heading into the barn to get to work. Mario had given him chores the day before, and he had things he needed to get done once he'd finished his chores, so in Marine style, he rolled up his proverbial sleeves and began.

He must have worked for an hour or more before he heard anyone else around him. "Have you done all this already?" Wally asked from behind him, and Gordon tried to hide his surprise. People used to be unable to sneak up on him. "The stalls look good. The others just need to be spot-cleaned. The horses aren't spending much time in them right now."

"I wanted to get done because Mario said we'd clean out the extra room, and then I need to help you with the cages for your cats." Gordon felt excitement at the thought of helping Wally build those enclosures. It would be the least he could do to make up for his actions. As Marines, you owned up to your mistakes and tried to make them right. In Gordon's mind, this would help make what he'd done that first night right.

"Then finish up here. I have some calls to make, and this afternoon we can head into town and pick up some of the supplies we need to get started," Wally said before clapping Gordon lightly on the shoulder. "Breakfast will be ready in an hour, so just come on inside." Wally walked away, and a few minutes later Gordon heard a truck engine start and then soften as it pulled into the distance. He kept working, and in an hour, went into the main house. It was quiet and he felt a bit like he shouldn't be here, but Wally had said he could.

"Morning, Gordon," Dakota said as he wandered into the living room. "Wally got a call, so you'll have to eat my cooking."

"Why don't you get someone to help? You both work all day and help run the ranch. There's no need to be cooking too." Without thinking, Gordon got up and went into the kitchen. He found the pans and opened the refrigerator, pulling out breakfast food. He chopped onions and broccoli, cut mushrooms, and cracked eggs.

"That smells heavenly," Dakota said a while later. Gordon looked up from his preparations and saw a cleaned and pressed man ready for work. He poured some of the egg mixture into the pan and waited a few minutes before flipping it. Once the omelet was done, he slid it onto a plate and set the plate on the table. Gordon heard Dakota sigh and then make happy noises as he ate. "Where did you learn to cook like this?"

"No idea. I found out I was good at it during basic, and after that, I sort of cooked on special occasions for the guys. The military food isn't really that bad, but you never get anything really out of the ordinary. I sort of made up recipes out of the MREs we'd get. Used the ingredients in those to make up something different," Gordon explained and then went back to the stove and began cooking another omelet when he heard the door open and close.

"Morning, Gordon," Haven said as he slid into the chair next to Dakota and instantly began talking about his plans for the next few weeks. Gordon brought him a plate. Haven took a bite and stopped talking. Dakota set down his fork and began to laugh.

"Your food must be good if you got him quiet," Dakota teased, and Gordon brought a plate for Phillip. "Wally's on a call and it was his turn to make breakfast, but Gordon stepped in." Dakota flashed him a smile.

Gordon was about to sit down to his own meal when Mario came in. He set his plate down in front of Mario and made a final omelet before joining the others at the table. "Damn, this is good," Mario said with a grin at him from across the table before returning to his food.

"I see someone cooked," Wally said as he came in. Gordon was about to get up again when Wally said, "I can wait a few minutes until you're done eating," then filled a mug before joining everyone at the table. As Gordon finished his breakfast, he saw Wally and Dakota exchanging silent looks. Those two were up to something, and by the way they glanced at him every few seconds, whatever their collective minds were up to involved him. Once he'd finished eating, Gordon got up, taking his coffee with him. He mixed up the last of the omelet mixture and made one for Wally, then placed his plate in front of him.

"How did the call go?" Dakota asked before sipping his coffee.

"Not too bad. Just a worried rancher," Wally answered, and Gordon actually saw him roll his eyes once in pleasure as he ate. Conversation around the table picked up, and Gordon began cleaning up.

"I'll help," Mario said, grabbing the dishcloth and hip-checking him away from the sink. Mario began washing the dishes, and Wally grabbed a towel, drying and then putting everything away. "That was wonderful," Mario said with a warm smile as he continued working. Gordon figured he'd best get out of the way, so he sat back down at the table while the others talked for a while. Then, one by one, they filtered out and got back to work. Gordon figured he had enough work to do, so he placed his mug silently by the sink and left the house.

He meant to go back to the barn, but ended up stopping at one of the paddocks to watch the horses. He didn't mean to stay long, but sort of lost track of time.

"What are you doing?" Mario asked from behind him, and Gordon silently cursed at being caught doing nothing.

"Just watching the horses," Gordon answered honestly. "Sometimes peace and quiet were impossible to find when I was… over there. I dreamed of times like this, when everything was peaceful without people crying or shooting at each other." Gordon turned slightly so he could watch Mario out of the corner of his eye. "I promised myself when I was there that if I ever found a place that was quiet and happy, I wouldn't take it for granted again." Gordon moved away from the rail fencing. "I'll get back to work."

"Wally asked if we'd make a run into town to pick up some of the supplies he needs. He'd go with us, but he just got another call. So, do you mind?" Mario asked.

"Nope. Do I need to bring anything?"

"Just get in the truck and we'll get going. I've got his list." Mario patted his pocket. Gordon followed him to the truck, and soon they were speeding down the road.

THE town wasn't large, but Gordon had gotten used to where everything was over the past few days since starting to work on the ranch. Mario pulled up in front of the hardware store, and they got out. He and Mario spent the next hour buying concrete and fencing supplies. He loaded them in the back of the truck while Mario did some additional shopping.

While he was working, Gordon saw a small group of four men in uniform walking down the sidewalk. They went into the armed forces recruiting office, and the day he signed up for the Marines flashed through his mind. Gordon finished loading the last of the concrete mix, and as he hoisted the truck lift gate into place, the men came out of the recruiting office, pressed young officers, probably getting ready to go on their first assignments. All of them looked across the street to where he stood. Old habits died hard, and Gordon was just about to salute when he stopped his hand, keeping it by his side.

"It's okay," Mario said, surprising him yet again. Gordon had to do something about this disappearing into his own head all the time.

"I don't want them to know I was a Marine," Gordon said, and then he wished he hadn't. "I got everything loaded. Is there anything else we need to do?" He hoped he'd changed the subject fast enough.

"Let's go, then," Mario said, and they both climbed into the truck for the ride back to the ranch. "Why don't you want people to know about your service?" Mario asked when they were just outside of town.

"I really don't want to talk about it. I'm trying to move on." Gordon knew his excuse probably sounded really lame, but he wasn't up for explanations of things he didn't want to remember and facts he wasn't really sure of. "That's my past."

"But it's something you should be proud of," Mario said.

Gordon knew Mario was right, and wished he could feel that way. But he didn't deserve to feel proud of what he'd done. He was convinced of that, and he wanted to forget and move on. "I just want to let the memories fade, and try to build a life."

"Okay," Mario said. "That's within your rights, and if that's what you want, I'll try to help as best I can." There was that smile again, reaching all the way to Mario's eyes. They rode quietly for a while, the only sounds the wind from the open windows and the hum of the tires on the hot road.

"Can I ask you a question?" Gordon asked, and Mario nodded. "Who's the man with you in the pictures in the living room? Is that your brother?"

Mario shook his head before glancing over at him. "I should probably have taken those down a while ago. That's David. He and I were together for a while, but he left about eighteen months ago." Mario sighed softly and returned his attention to driving.

They turned quiet again, and Gordon peered out the windows, watching the rangeland whiz by. "I didn't mean to upset you." Gordon understood that a man sometimes had things he didn't want to talk about. He turned away from the side window. "There are just so many pictures around."

Mario groaned softly. "I know. David and I were together for over three years, and then he got this job offer that he said was too good to pass up, and he left. But I'm not dumb. David was younger than me, and he followed some guy to greener pastures." Mario sighed. "I feel sort of pathetic, if you want to know the truth. I thought David was the guy I'd be with for the long haul."

"So you kept the pictures around because you hoped he'd come back?" Gordon asked and wondered why his stomach tightened a little.

"Yes and no, I guess. David's gone and it isn't likely he's ever coming back. He's called a few times, mostly to make sure I'm okay, but he has a new life with someone else, and I've known for a while that I needed to move on. I guess with the pictures around, I didn't feel quite so lonely." Mario scoffed as he looked across the seat. "Sounds kind of dumb, I know, but sometimes out here, life can be lonely, especially when most of the people around you are paired up already." Mario quieted, and Gordon couldn't think of anything to add, so they rode on and eventually turned into the ranch drive, pulling up near the barn.

Gordon didn't open his door right away, instead pulling out his wallet. Carefully, he withdrew a picture of three men, looking at it for a second before passing it to Mario. "I understand about keeping pictures of people you care about around to not feel so lonely." Mario took the photograph, and Gordon watched as he looked at it. Gordon knew the picture of Stacks, Bottles, and him from memory. "That was taken a long time ago in Afghanistan. All three of us were so young then, and we all thought we were going to change the world and make it a safer place for everyone." Gordon leaned over the seat. "The tall one is Warren, we called him Stacks, and the man on the other side of me is Robert. We called him Bottles, because when we enlisted they gave him regulation glasses and they were so damned thick." Gordon laughed slightly at the memory.

"Did they have a nickname for you?" Mario asked, still looking at the picture.

"I was Canoe because of my huge feet." Gordon grinned, wriggling his toes in his boots. "I haven't thought about that in a while. My nickname didn't really stick and everyone called me Gordon or Gord, but the other two, their nicknames stuck forever. I have to think about their real names, because they'll always be

Stacks and Bottles in my mind." Mario handed him back the picture, and Gordon gingerly placed it back in his wallet.

"I remember you said Stacks never got to meet his daughter, but do you ever see Bottles?" Mario asked.

Gordon swallowed hard. "I was the only one in that picture who made it home." Buried memories tried to come to the surface, but he shoved them back into the box and made sure they were locked away tight.

"I'm sorry. Do you see any of the other guys in your unit?" Mario shifted on the seat.

"Yeah. Sometimes. Lately, though, the phone calls have tapered off. I suppose most of the guys have lives and families of their own to worry about," Gordon said. And it wasn't as though he was heating up the phone lines with his own calls to see how everyone was doing, so he couldn't blame them. The blame rested with him, he knew that. But there wasn't any way he could face those guys again after what had happened.

"I suppose people grow apart. Distance and time tend to take their toll," Mario said before opening the truck door and climbing out. Gordon did the same, closing the truck door with a bang before walking around to the back. "Is there a special place you want me to put all this stuff?"

"There should be room in the equipment shed," Mario answered before hoisting a bag of concrete. Gordon did the same and followed Mario. Together they unloaded all the supplies from the truck.

"Thanks, guys," Wally called as he hurried by, with Liam right behind him. "I'm on a call. There's sandwich stuff in the fridge—help yourselves when you're ready to eat." He barely stopped walking while he talked, and soon his truck was speeding down the drive and then making the turn onto the road.

"I sort of feel like a fool," Gordon muttered softly. Mario stopped what he was doing. "I believed those people when they said

Wally and Dakota were mistreating the animals in their care. They seemed so sincere and passionate, and I guess I got caught up. I should know better."

"Fanatics are really good at drawing people to their causes. Right or wrong, they truly believe whatever cause they've taken up. Facts don't matter, only emotion and extreme passion. It's easy to get caught up in that," Mario said as he moved closer. "I don't mean anything by this, so don't take it the wrong way, but it's easy to get pulled in when you're living out of your car and aren't sure where your next meal is coming from."

"At least I was on my own and not sponging off anyone," Gordon said, his defenses rising regardless of what Mario had said.

"I wasn't judging, just maybe stating that your decision-making processes probably weren't at their peak. You wouldn't make that same decision now, would you?" Mario asked, and Gordon shook his head. "That was all I was saying. You were trying to survive, and they offered you a lifeline of sorts. I'd have probably taken it too, in your position."

Gordon straightened his stance. "I was a Marine. I should know better."

Mario clapped him lightly on the shoulder. "You're also human and allowed the same flaws and failings as the rest of us. You know better and are working with the sheriff to help catch those guys. You're making things right. That's all you can do now."

Gordon narrowed his eyes. "Why are you being so understanding? My sergeant would have kicked my ass from here to kingdom come if he knew what I'd done." Mario shrugged his answer, saying nothing, but Gordon felt his gaze on him, and damn if he didn't like the way that felt. Mario moved a little bit closer. The air around Gordon seemed charged with electricity. He wanted to know the taste of Mario's skin and the feel of Mario's work-roughened hands on his bare skin rather than through his shirt, but he couldn't. Mario deserved a whole man, not one that was broken… not one who'd done what he did.

"I'm not your sergeant, so what he would have done doesn't matter, and as for being understanding, just wait until you mess up something really important. Then you'll see just how understanding I am. Now, the work isn't going to do itself, and we still have that room to clean out. So go on in and eat fast so you can get back at it." Mario strode off, and Gordon walked into the house.

He easily found the sandwich fixings and made two, eating them fast before heading back out toward the barn where he finished up his chores. Once he was done, he tried to find Mario, but he was nowhere around, so Gordon wandered around to the back of the house to get a better look at the enclosures. He didn't get too close, but he wanted to see how they were constructed. Trees had been planted around the enclosures for shade, and Gordon saw where another stand had been planted away from the others. That was obviously where Wally planned to build the next set of enclosures.

"I see you figured out where I want to build," Wally called as he strode over to where Gordon was standing.

"It wasn't hard. You want to provide them with some shade," Gordon said. "Will there be four cages like in the other groupings?"

"Yes. That's the first one we built, and I want this enclosure a bit larger. That way I can move some of the existing animals in here for more room, depending on what I get. I do want a larger exercise area for them," Wally said as he began pacing off the outline.

"How'd you decide to start doing this? I mean, it's a huge commitment in time and money."

Wally laughed. "Just insane, I guess, or that's what Dakota used to think. When we met, he and I had very different ideas about how animals should be treated. To a degree, we still do. He understands about the cats and stuff." Wally shook his head slowly. "When Dakota and I first met, we had a difference of opinion about some wolves. Dakota was having some problems with them, and well, I kind of rescued an injured one and nursed it back to health. Dakota nearly came unglued when he found out, or more accurately, came face to face with an injured wolf in the old shed." Wally pointed to the west. "It used to be right over there, but we tore it down a while ago."

"Do you still have wolf problems?"

"That's why Dakota doesn't mind the cats. When the lions hear a wolf cry, they tend to answer with a roar, and that has the tendency to keep the wolves away. Schian was the best wolf repellant, and Shahrazad would howl loud enough to curl your hair. Between those two, they scared the wolves half to death. Some showed up a few years ago, but it's been a while since we've heard any in the area." Wally stopped what he was doing. "Did Mario say when he thought we would be able to get started?"

"I got my chores done for the day," Gordon said.

"There's string and stakes in the equipment shed. We can get the dimensions measured and staked so Mario can bring out the backhoe and dig the trenches for the foundations." Wally was already hurrying away, and Gordon's phone rang. "You go ahead and get that. I'll be right back with the supplies." Wally continued hurrying away as Gordon fished out his phone. He didn't recognize the number and almost didn't answer, but his curiosity got the better of him.

"Hello," Gordon said a bit tentatively.

"Gord!" an excited voice said on the other end of the line. "It's Greeves."

Gordon smiled big—speak of the devil. "God, Greeves, it's good to hear your voice. Where are you? Still deployed or back in the States?"

"I opted out when my hitch was up. Figured I'd spend some time with the family while I figure things out. Hadn't been out two weeks and I had recruiters knocking on my door trying to get me to sign up for another hitch. Told them no thanks."

"You sound happy," Gordon said, wandering into the shade of one of the trees.

"I am. A bit at loose ends, but it's nice to spend time with my sons. When I got home, they didn't know who I was." There was a touch of sadness in his voice. "The youngest screamed whenever I held him. But things are better now. Can't believe the highlight of my day is taking the kids for a walk in the stroller." He paused for a few seconds. "How are you?"

"Figuring things out, been working on a—"

"Don't tell me," Greeves interrupted. "It's better if I don't know."

"Know what?"

"Some guys from the Navy stopped by a day or so ago and were asking if I knew where you were. Don't know what they wanted. You know the type—desk jockeys that talked in Navy-speak and asked all their questions like there was a stick shoved eight miles up their ass. I told them I didn't know where you were. Didn't then and I still don't. I got your number from Stacks's wife, and she said she didn't know where you were or if the number was still good."

"Thanks. I don't know what they want, either," Gordon said honestly, but official types were never good, especially when they were self-important desk jockeys. Whatever they wanted, Gordon was glad Greeves hadn't said anything. "But I'm grateful."

"We'll always have each other's backs, you know that. If I can, I'll call some buddies and see if I can find out what they want. It could be something good," Greeves said, and two seconds later, they both broke into laughter. They'd found out long ago that if anyone in the military was looking for you in any way, it was not a good thing. "You take care, and if you're ever in Virginia, we'd all love to see you."

"Once I have my head on straight, I'll have to make the trip to see you," Gordon said. They talked for a few minutes more and then hung up.

"Good news?" Wally asked as he handed Gordon the stakes and a hammer. "You're smiling like a kid."

"Just a friend from my unit," Gordon said before shoving his phone in his pocket and schooling the expression on his face. "He called to see how I was doing."

"It's always good to talk with old friends," Wally said as he moved around the clearing. "I think I want the far corner here," he said, indicating the spot with his foot.

"Don't we need to measure to find the best spot?" Gordon asked as he set down the stakes and began driving one where Wally indicated.

Wally snickered. "We're not building the pyramids, so we don't need to orient them to the sun. What I want is as much shade for the enclosure as possible. It makes it a lot easier on the cats. The exact orientation of the enclosures is less important." Wally then began to move down what appeared to be a line in his head. "Thirty feet this way," he said almost to himself, and Gordon measured out the string and held it for Wally. "A little more that way." Gordon moved the string. "Perfect. Stake that, and we'll have the baseline we can use to lay out the rest of it."

Gordon was glad Wally knew what he was doing because he seemed to fly by the seat of his pants, and yet as he followed Wally's instructions, the enclosure took shape—like the other one, only larger. Gordon checked the angles to make sure each corner was square and that each stake was in its exact spot. Once the outside dimensions were laid out, they began filling in the center areas. He was glad for the exacting work; it kept his mind off the phone call from Greeves and his curiosity about what the service could want from him. Not that he had any intention of finding out if he could help it. He'd been off the grid for a while. His phone was one that he prepaid the minutes to use, and he always did that with cash. He had no bills or address, got no checks or mail, nothing. They'd lose interest in whatever they wanted and look for someone else after a while. He hadn't done anything wrong, so he sort of figured they wanted him to re-up or some such nonsense, and he had no intention of doing that, not in a million years. He'd done his bit and given more than his pound of flesh for his country—physically, mentally, and emotionally—and that was more than enough.

"You okay?" Wally asked, and Gordon realized he'd been standing staring at nothing for a while.

"Sorry," Gordon said and went back to work, pushing the conversation with Greeves out of his mind.

"I THINK that's all we can do for today," Wally proclaimed an hour later as they stood reviewing their handiwork. Gordon nodded and stayed quiet. If Wally was happy, then he was happy.

"Looks like you're ready to start building," Mario said as he came up to stand next to Gordon. "If it doesn't rain, we should be able to get the foundations dug and the concrete set tomorrow."

"I hope so. It needs time to cure before we can start building the enclosures themselves, and this has to be ready before the animals arrive."

"It will be," Gordon promised as he looked toward the west. "We could bring in the digging equipment and get started."

"No," Wally said. "We've all worked hard enough, and overdoing it isn't going to get the job done any faster." Wally began picking up the extra stakes and string. "Go on, I'll be there in a minute."

Gordon reluctantly turned away and walked around the house with Mario. "Did I say something wrong?"

"No. Wally worries about his animals, even the ones he hasn't gotten yet. Tomorrow we'll get the foundation dug and poured with the posts set in it. After a few days, we'll be able to build the rest of the enclosure. It's the waiting that gets to him." Mario continued toward his place as they reached the front porch of the main house.

"Should I come with you?" Gordon asked.

"No. Dakota's probably making dinner. I'll be in soon. I've just got a few things to do before I call it a day." Mario strode away, and Gordon thought of following him anyway, but went inside instead. Dakota was working in the kitchen.

"Would you like a beer?" Dakota asked, handing him a bottle without waiting for an answer. "It's my night to cook, so the chances are we'll need some fortification."

"What are you planning for dinner?" Gordon asked as he accepted the beer.

"Don't really know," Dakota answered, and Gordon opened the beer, taking a swig before pulling open the refrigerator door. He began by getting out the makings for salad and then started a pot of rice. Gordon then looked through the cupboards and found the rest of the ingredients he needed.

"Looks like we're having stir-fry," Gordon said, taking another drink from his beer before getting down to work chopping the vegetables.

"Thanks," Dakota said with a distracted smile before turning back to the table. Gordon left him alone and continued working. Wally came in as Gordon finished the salad and set the bowl in the refrigerator. Then he got a pan hot and started cooking the small chunks of beef.

"Is something wrong?" Gordon heard Wally ask Dakota. He continued his cooking, enjoying the unstressful activity.

"I have a patient that's got me totally baffled," Dakota said from behind him. "He's dangerously overweight and I've put him on a regimen of diet and exercise. Both he and his mother swear he's following my instructions, but nothing is happening. In fact, he's gained weight somehow, and I'm worried about the stress on his heart and organs." Gordon peered over his shoulder and saw Dakota fiddling with his beer bottle as Wally sat down next to him. Then Wally jumped up and hurried out of the room. Gordon continued working and Wally rushed back with a magazine in his hand. He opened it and pointed out an article. "Dragonflies?" Dakota said.

"Kota, you know that dogs get cancer. Did you know that monkeys get heart disease or that whales can get Hodgkin's lymphoma? Animals and humans aren't that far apart. They get lots of the same diseases. There are wallabies and goats with substance abuse problems. They seek out specific plants for their drug properties. This entomologist discovered overweight dragonflies. He found out they had an infection that affected their ability to process food and they gained weight. Maybe your patient doesn't fit the diet-and-exercise model because there's something else wrong."

Dakota pulled Wally into a hug, holding him, and Wally held Dakota in return, the two of them simply resting in each other's arms. It was tender, kind, and beautiful. It also made Gordon's heart ache. He wanted that so badly—someone to help him with his problems and hold him when he wanted to say thank you. Dakota and Wally made no move to separate, and Gordon looked away, feeling like he was intruding. He returned to his cooking, adding the vegetables to the pan. He continued stirring before adding water chestnuts and bamboo shoots. He loved them for their crunch. Finally, he added soy sauce and turned down the heat, letting all the flavors come together.

"We should help Gordon," Wally said, and Dakota chuckled, releasing Wally from the hug.

Wally got the silverware, and Dakota the plates and glasses, while Gordon dished up the rice and placed the stir-fry into a bowl. Mario came in as he was finishing up. "I wasn't sure how many people would be here for dinner, so I made plenty," Gordon said. He needn't have worried, because a few minutes later, Haven and Phillip came in. Additional places were set, and Gordon sat next to Mario while everyone ate. Wally talked about the progress on the enclosure, and then the conversation shifted to plans for the coming days and weeks.

"Wonderful meal," Wally said, leaning back in his chair and lightly patting his belly. The others echoed the sentiment, and Gordon thanked them, standing up to take his plate to the sink. Mario's hand on his arm stopped him, and he sat back down.

"We'll clean up," Mario said, and the others began clearing the table. Dakota placed another beer in front of him, which Gordon opened, his eyes already getting heavy.

By the time he'd finished his beer, the others had cleaned up. Gordon said good night and left the house, wandering through the yard. "Come on," Mario said when he caught up with him, barely pausing as he strode toward his house. "I have a surprise for you." Mario led him inside and down the hall, pushing open the door to the extra room. "I cleaned it out. There isn't much."

Gordon looked inside. The room was sparse, with just a bed, dresser, and lamp, but Mario had made the bed with what looked like a handmade quilt. "Thank you," Gordon said softly. "It's been a while since I had a space that felt like home." Gordon turned to face Mario. "This was very nice of you." Gordon's stomach fluttered, and he wasn't sure if he should move closer to Mario or do everything he could to get away. It had been a while since anyone had done something to make him more comfortable, and it touched him in a way he hadn't expected.

"I didn't do much," Mario said with equal softness, and the spark between them that Gordon had felt once before crackled. "I want you to feel comfortable here. You can feel free to hang pictures if you like. The closet is empty too," Mario said as he moved away, opening the door. He sounded a bit nervous, and Gordon wondered if Mario felt the energy too. "You can get your things and put them away," Mario said, but Gordon wasn't really listening. His attention focused on the way Mario reached to the shelf in the closet to retrieve a box he must have missed. His shirt rode up and a strip of tanned skin showed above Mario's low-riding jeans. Gordon wanted to reach out and touch, but wasn't sure if the advance would be welcome. Hell, he wasn't sure of very damned much these days, and he hated that. He was a damned Marine. He'd seen combat and lived through shit that would kill other people, and yet the thought of losing someone else tore at him. He hated the weakness, especially in himself.

Screw it—he was a Marine, and you don't get anything unless you go for it. Pushing aside his reticence and doubt, Gordon moved forward, intent on sliding his hands along that strip of skin so he could finally get the feel of cowboy warmth on his hands. Gordon was right behind Mario, close enough he could feel the heat from his skin, when Mario's phone rang. Gordon backed away quietly as Mario pulled down the box and set it on the bed before fishing out his phone.

"David," Mario said excitedly, and Gordon closed his eyes, breathing a sigh of relief. "How are you?" Just from those few words and the energy in Mario's voice, Gordon understood the depth of feeling Mario still had for his ex. He wished someone cared for him that way. Mario scooped up the box from the bed, and after flashing a quick smile, left the room. Gordon closed the door and sat on the edge of the bed, his heart pounding. Maybe that was for the best. He certainly wasn't ready for anything, and Mario was still hung up on this David. At least he hadn't made a complete fool of himself. Gordon sat for a few minutes before getting up and heading outside to get his duffel from next to the sofa. "So you aren't really happy there?" Mario was asking, and Gordon saw the hope rising in Mario's eyes. He carried the bag back to his room and closed the door. He didn't need to hear any more.

Gordon unpacked his things, wondering if he wasn't being a fool. He hadn't meant to allow himself to develop feelings for Mario, and yet somehow it had happened. Granted, they were very new, and he vowed to snuff them out. Mario's heart was set on another, and even if he couldn't have David, Gordon knew he couldn't compete with a memory. Leaving the room, he heard Mario still talking animatedly on the phone. He ignored the conversation and brought in the rest of his things from the car and unpacked them before cleaning up. When he came out of the bathroom, he didn't hear Mario on the phone any longer and the house was quiet. He listened for Mario, but heard nothing. After closing his door behind him, Gordon got ready for bed and slipped beneath the crisp bedding.

He hoped he wouldn't wake Mario with his nightmares again, and in the early morning, with the sun just beginning to shine through the window, Gordon realized he hadn't dreamed once of the war or what had happened. All he remembered were his dreams of Mario, lascivious dreams that left him sweaty and panting in the night. Dreams of someone he couldn't have. Maybe it would have been better to dream about bullets, sand, heat, and war. At least he knew what to do when that happened, but this left him empty and alone.

MARIO hung up the phone and sat unmoving on the sofa. He really wished he knew why he continually did this to himself. His phone had rung, David had called to talk, and Mario had felt his heart race from the first sound of David's deep, rich voice. Of course, like the other times, David was just being friendly, but Mario couldn't keep his hopes from rising, and now, once again, he'd gotten his hopes dashed.

Mario heard Gordon moving around at the other end of the house, and his thoughts ran to the other man. Here was a sexy, gorgeous man that Mario had seen watching him more than once, who also caught his interest. But as soon as David called, Mario was ready to hurry away just to talk to him. *It's pathetic—I'm pathetic.* Mario looked around the living room and saw David's smiling face looking back at him from at least a dozen different picture frames, David alone, David and him at the beach, on horseback. The picture David let him take sitting naked on a horse, the pommel covering his…. He had to stop all this. Mario stood up and quietly moved through the room, picking up the pictures and then placing them in a pile on one end of the sofa. He pulled the ones down off the walls and added them to the stack as well. He was never going to get over David unless he removed him from every place he looked.

He carried the pictures quietly down the hall and into his bedroom, opened the bottom drawer of his dresser, and placed them inside. After that, he packed up the pictures of him and David from his dresser and nightstand, adding them to the stash and then closing the drawer. Then Mario sat on the edge of his bed, trying to see if he felt better, or at least different.

It was time he moved on—he knew that. David was gone and he wasn't coming back. Mario still had feelings for him, but that was his problem. It had been a while, and Mario was convinced more than ever that the reason he wasn't over David and able to move on was because he wasn't willing to let go. Well, he had to, starting now. Mario stood up and walked quietly to the bathroom and got cleaned up. As he walked back down the hall to go to bed, he stopped outside Gordon's door when he heard talking. Mario was afraid Gordon might have been having a nightmare and expected him to scream. He did cry out, but what Mario heard stilled him instantly. Mario thought he might have been hearing things, but it came again, this time clear as a bell. He thought about knocking to make sure Gordon was all right, but thought better of it and backed away from the door before heading to his room. Mario closed his door and got undressed, then climbed under the covers, still wondering why Gordon would be calling out his name.

Chapter Four

"MORNING, Gordon," Mario said as he approached where he stood leaning on the rail, watching the horses. Whenever Gordon took a break, Mario always knew where to find him—right in this spot.

"Hey," Gordon said with a small, brief smile before going back to watching the horses again. Over the past week, since Mario had heard Gordon calling his name, they hadn't really spoken much other than about work. Mario asked Gordon to do things, and he always did them to the best of his ability, but they didn't talk about anything else. Before that, Mario had thought they were on their way to being friends at least, but that seemed to have ended, and Mario wondered why but he'd been afraid to ask. His own feelings for Gordon were muddled at best.

"Have you been sleeping okay?" Mario asked, trying to find something that Gordon would talk about, but he'd been withdrawn and quiet for days.

"Yes, thanks," Gordon said without even turning to look at him. Then, after a few moments, Gordon stepped away from the fence. "I need to make breakfast." Gordon strode toward the house like he had some place to go in a hurry.

Mario shook his head and walked off toward the barn. Lately, most mornings he stayed away from the house, grabbing a bite from his own refrigerator instead. Mario loaded one of the trucks with the fencing for Wally's cat enclosure and drove it out behind the house, unloading it near where they were working before getting ready to drive back around.

"Get in here and eat," Wally called, and Mario sighed before giving in and walking toward the house. "Gordon made egg sandwiches and they're amazing," Wally told him as he held the back door for him, closing it once he was inside. Mario took a seat, and Gordon brought him a plate but refused to meet his eyes. "What's going on?" Wally whispered, and Mario shrugged, shaking his head before taking a bite.

"Damn, this is good," he said, smiling at Gordon, who nodded, but didn't look at him.

Wally finished up what he was eating and got up, placing his plate in the sink. "I got a call," he said, leaning toward Dakota for a kiss. He said something Mario couldn't hear and then left the room with Dakota following close behind.

"Those two are up to something," Gordon said as he added another sandwich to Mario's plate and then sat at the table with his own.

Mario agreed and swallowed a bite of his sandwich. "Did I do something to piss you off?" Mario asked. "You haven't said more than two words to me all week."

"No," Gordon said.

"See, there's one word," Mario prodded, figuring a little poking might get the bear to open up. "What crawled up your butt? And why are you taking it out on me?"

"I'm fine. Just feel like being quiet, that's all," Gordon said, but Mario didn't feel like letting it go.

"There's more to it and you know it. I've seen you talking to Wally for hours while you worked on the enclosures, and you and Phillip sat on the porch two days ago and you never shut up. I heard your voice and laughter inside the house all evening. It's me you won't talk to, and I think I deserve an explanation." Mario put down the sandwich he was holding and stared at Gordon. "If I've done something, then you owe it to me as a man to say something." Mario saw Gordon swallow hard, but he still didn't say anything. "Fine," Mario stood up and left the table, walking out the back door. He strode to the truck and drove back around to the front, where he saw Gordon standing on the porch, staring at him. Mario got out of the truck and watched as Gordon walked toward him. He waited for Gordon to come closer and expected some explanation.

What Mario got was what he least expected—kissed within an inch of his life. Mario could hardly breathe as Gordon covered his mouth, cupping the sides of his head in his hands. This was no gentle peck, but a full-on, breath-stealing, lips-smashing, damned near brain-sucking kiss that left Mario unable to think. He could barely react for a second, and then he was kissing Gordon back, crushing the other man to him. Damn it, if Gordon was going to kiss him, Mario was going to kiss him back.

Without waiting for an invitation, Gordon parted his lips, and Mario surged his tongue forward, taking possession of the larger man's mouth. He wanted this, had wanted this for quite a while, and damn it all, he was going to get all he could.

Their lips parted in a mutual gasp, and then Mario heaved a deep breath, staring into Gordon's eyes. He wasn't sure if Gordon planned to back away and try to pretend their kiss didn't happen or not, but Mario wasn't going to give him a chance. Pulling him forward, he crushed their bodies together and took possession of Gordon's full lips. He tasted good, and Mario feasted on him, kissing, nibbling.

"We shouldn't do this," Gordon said when Mario pulled away.

"We sure as hell should," Mario growled. He was damned near ready to strip Gordon naked on Wally and Dakota's front porch and take him right here, right now. But he backed away, breathing deeply, like he'd just run a race. Gordon looked around, presumably to see if anyone was watching. "Everyone on this ranch, gay or not, has seen two men kissing more than once."

"But you're the foreman, and this isn't the place to be showing everyone our business," Gordon said, backing away and straightening his clothes.

Mario agreed, but parts of him were more than ready to override good sense. Breathing deeply, he put a little more distance between them and tried to clear his head. "Is that what the last week has been all about?"

Gordon nodded. "Not that it really matters," Gordon said before turning around.

"What the hell does that mean?" Mario asked, grabbing Gordon's arm to stop him.

Gordon turned back to him. "It doesn't matter how I feel or what I want. Yes, I have feelings for you, and they're all jumbled up, but it doesn't mean shit because you're still hung up on David." Gordon stood stock-still. "I keep seeing you in my dreams at night and think about you all the time. But I heard you on the phone with David when he called. You're still in love with him, so how I feel or what I want doesn't mean crap. You're hung up on a man who's gone, and I can't change your heart." Gordon shrugged and pulled his arm away before walking toward the barn. "Please leave me alone, I have work to get done."

Mario was stunned. That was the only way he could describe it. His legs didn't seem to be able to move, but he followed every movement of Gordon's ramrod-straight body until he disappeared into the barn.

"Got yourself in a bit of a pickle, don't you?" Wally said as he descended the stairs, carrying a mug of coffee.

"I thought you were on a call," Mario said, instantly realizing he'd been set up by matchmaker Wally. The man was the biggest yenta Mario had ever seen.

"I'm about to leave." Wally continued to his truck. "I'm just waiting for Liam." Wally sipped from his travel mug. "That was some lip-lock you had each other in."

"You saw that?" Mario asked.

Wally chuckled. "Half the county either saw it or felt the static electricity. So what's the problem?"

"Gordon's attracted, that was plainly obvious." Mario touched his still tingling lips without thinking about it. "But he said it doesn't matter because I'm still hung up on David."

"Are you?" Wally asked with raised eyebrows. "David's gone and he's not coming back. It's sad that the relationship ended—you seemed so good together—but it did. Not everything works out."

"Says the man who has everything," Mario chided a bit jealously. He wanted what Wally and Dakota had, and he'd thought he had that with David.

"Let me ask you this. Are you hanging onto David because you're afraid of getting involved with someone else and getting hurt again?" Wally asked as a truck pulled into the drive. Liam parked off to the side and then joined Wally. "Think about it." Wally and Liam got in the truck, and soon they were off on their call. Mario watched them go, trying to come up with the answer to Wally's question. The truth was he didn't know what in hell he felt. David was gone, and he was trying to move on, but the empty place in his heart was still there and had never healed. Mario turned and saw Gordon moving around inside the barn. Without thinking, he walked toward him.

Gordon continued working and appeared to be trying to ignore him, but Mario walked into the barn and right next to where Gordon was working. "Yes, I still have feelings for David. He and I were together for over three years, but that's over. David isn't coming back and I want to move on."

Gordon stopped pitching dirty horse bedding into the wheelbarrow. "I noticed that all the pictures were gone," Gordon began. "But I also heard how excited you were when he called."

"Didn't you ever have a person who got under your skin and you could never seem to get them out no matter how bad you wanted to? David's like that for me, or at least he was."

"What's changed in a week?" Gordon asked skeptically.

"I don't know," Mario answered.

Gordon leaned on the handle of the shovel he was using. "If David walked through that door today, what would you do?"

Mario followed Gordon's gaze and realized he didn't know the answer. He shrugged slowly. "I don't know."

Gordon lifted the shovel and went back to work. "I suggest you come back when you know the answer."

Mario didn't know what to say to that and turned to leave. "Wally's on a call. When he comes back, we're going to set the fencing on his enclosures."

"I'll be done here," Gordon said without looking up from his work. Knowing it would be futile to talk anymore, Mario left the barn and saw Haven pulling into the drive.

"You got a few minutes?" Haven asked.

"Sure," Mario answered and followed him to the porch, where they went over the plans for the next week. There was plenty to do, including moving one of the herds to fresh range and then walking and repairing the fences in that area. As they finished up, a sheriff's vehicle pulled into the drive and parked next to Mario's truck.

"Did you find them?" Mario asked as a deputy got out of the cruiser.

"Not yet. We've had a few leads, but they seem one step ahead of us. I was wondering if we could talk to"—he consulted his notes—"Gordon for a few minutes?"

"He's in the barn," Mario said, and after making sure there was nothing else Haven needed, he led the deputy to where Gordon was working.

"Do you have news?" Gordon asked.

"Not much. We were hoping you could tell us if they mentioned where they might be staying or how you were to get in touch with them. The group seems to have disappeared from the area."

Gordon thought for few minutes and then shook his head. "We met at the diner, and they didn't talk much except about their cause. I never went back to the hotel with them or anything like that, and I was supposed to meet them back at the diner the following day to tell them how things went. Of course I never showed, but I already told that to the sheriff." The deputy nodded slowly and made notes. "If I think of anything or see any of them again, I'll be sure to let you know."

"Everything been quiet?" the deputy asked as he turned to Mario.

"Yeah. There haven't been other incidents. If they're smart, they realized Gordon gave them up and they probably skipped the area."

The deputy scoffed. "I'd like to think so, but fanatics can do things you don't expect. Keep an eye out and call us if you see or hear anything." He closed his notebook and headed toward the car. Mario and Gordon watched him go, and then Gordon returned to his work without saying a word.

Mario wanted to scream, and figured a good old fashioned, all-out fight was preferable to being ignored. But Dakota wouldn't stand for it, so Mario huffed and went to finish his work.

AFTER lunch, Wally and Liam returned from their calls, and together with Mario and Gordon, they started stringing the fencing on the enclosure. It was a big job, because the metal fencing had to be strung on top of the enclosure as well as on the sides, and special drops had to be constructed for feeding, along with sliding gates to close off specific areas of the enclosure. "Will we be able to finish today?" Wally asked, smearing a streak of dirt as he wiped his forehead.

"We should get close," Mario said as he finished making up one of the sliding gates. "I've got one more gate to do." Mario looked around and saw Gordon working, with his shirt off, to secure all the fencing to the posts and roof supports. Without meaning to, he watched as Gordon reached over his head, using pliers to fasten the fencing. Jeans rode low on Gordon's hips, and as he inhaled, his stomach pulled in, creating deep muscle lines that disappeared into Gordon's jeans. Fuck, Mario wanted to follow those lines and see where they led.

"If you two would quit dancing around each other," Wally whispered, shaking his head as he finished checking that the base of the fence was taut and strong enough that the cats couldn't bend it to get out. Every inch of the enclosure had to be tested and retested, because any weakness would be exploited and could mean a potentially dangerous animal could get loose.

"Yenta," Mario whispered, and Wally rolled his eyes even as Mario continued watching Gordon. Damn he was gorgeous: strong arms, bulging chest, and a light treasure trail that led south from his belly button. Pulling his eyes away, Mario slid the gate home, locking it in place. "Smooth as silk," Mario said happily, and he began work on the last divider, but he kept getting distracted, and when Gordon turned around, Mario groaned softly. He loved watching Gordon work. His muscles stretched and bulged as he moved, but it made for a huge distraction.

"Let's call it a day. We can finish tomorrow," Wally said, putting down his tools. "It's hot, and I'm exhausted."

"There isn't much left to do. Gordon and I can finish, and you can check over everything tomorrow," Mario said, wondering if this was another of Wally's yenta tricks.

"Thanks," Wally said, wiping his forehead again before he picked up his tools and walked slowly toward the house.

Mario got to work on the remaining gate, cutting the fencing to size with the pliers and then fastening it to the frame, while Gordon continued working above his head, fastening the fencing to the frame there. Mario wasn't getting much done, spending most of his time watching Gordon instead. Finally, he set his work aside and stood up, stretching in the heat. His shirt stuck to his skin, so Mario tugged it off, the air fresh on his skin. Mario walked over to Gordon and stood close, watching him work.

"What are you doing?" Gordon asked as he crimped one of the fasteners.

"What I've been doing all afternoon," he said and ran his hand lightly down Gordon's back. "Wondering just how wonderful this would feel." Mario moved closer. "I've watched you all afternoon," he whispered.

"Mario," Gordon protested with no heat. "I won't be someone's plaything or some rebound guy you try to bury your feelings with."

"You aren't," Mario said, and Gordon finished what he was doing, lowering his arms before turning to face him.

"How do you know?" Gordon challenged, and Mario stepped closer, cupping Gordon's cheeks and pulling him into a kiss. Words sucked. He was terrible at words when it came to telling people how he felt. Everything got muddled between his brain and his mouth, so he let his lips do the talking in a way he knew would come across crystal clear. Mario kissed Gordon with everything he had and heard him moan softly and felt him kiss back. He heard tools drop to the ground, and then Gordon held him tight, pressing their hips and chests together.

Mario felt Gordon slide his hand up his stomach to his chest, and it was Mario's turn to moan softly when Gordon lightly plucked one of his nipples. "Jesus," he whimpered against Gordon's lips, arching his back as Gordon intensified the sensation briefly before pulling his hand back. Their kiss intensified and turned into a battle for dominance. Their tongues dueled and they lightly nipped at each other's lips with their teeth. Mario was used to being in charge, but it appeared Gordon wasn't giving an inch. Whenever Mario pressed, he got back double from Gordon. "If you think I'm some sort of pushover—" Gordon growled, pressing Mario back a step with his weight.

"I'm glad to see you've kissed and made up, or whatever it was you were doing," Wally said with a chuckle from behind Mario, and he jumped back slightly. "But I don't think you need to give everyone a show." Mario felt himself blush and then cursed softly under his breath.

Gordon backed away and looked at the ground around him before snatching his shirt off the grass and pulling it on. "No. We certainly didn't," he said gruffly, and then he returned to his work.

"Dinner will be ready in an hour," Wally told them with mischief in his voice as he walked back to the house. Mario thanked him and returned to work as well.

"You know he was teasing," Mario told Gordon, who grunted.

"I figured, but still…." Gordon picked up another fastener. "Some things shouldn't be done for all the world to see." Gordon put the heavy strip of wire in place and began to fasten it. "Some things are private and should stay that way."

"Okay, I can agree with that. I'm not usually into displays and stuff," Mario said, returning to fastening the fencing to the divider.

"You could have fooled me," Gordon sniped.

"Hey, I wasn't alone either time, you know," Mario countered, and Gordon nodded as he continued working.

"There was a guy in my unit, we called him Bear because his real name was Teddy. He loved the ladies and had a stunner hanging on his arm every chance he got. Thing was, those women quickly found out they were like one of Teddy's belts or a pair of shoes, an accessory to go with his outfit. He always made big displays of affection with them when anyone was around, because that was part of the bling that went with having a buxom blonde on your arm. Didn't like it then, and I don't now."

"Okay. I'll remember that," Mario said, and he reminded himself that there was no prohibition mentioned once the doors were closed. "What happened to Teddy?" Mario asked as he continued working.

"He mustered out about a year ago and I haven't heard much about him," Gordon said. "Probably up to his old tricks and still will be when he's in a wheelchair in the nursing home." Gordon laughed as he continued working. "The guy was a real piece of work. Great guy to have fun with, but if you were a woman, you needed to avoid him like the plague." Gordon got another fastener.

They worked quietly for a while, but Mario found he kept watching Gordon as opposed to getting his work done. Pulling his gaze away from where he'd been staring at Gordon's tight bubble butt, he got to work and finished the divider, trying it out and then locking it in place. Then he helped Gordon with the last of the fasteners. The light was fading as they gathered their tools and walked together toward the house.

"You're almost late for dinner," Wally said with a smile as they approached.

"But we got it finished," Gordon said with a grin as Mario followed him inside. They hurried to wash up and then joined the group of people at the table.

"Gordon, I don't believe you've met Steve and Wilson," Wally said, and Mario watched Gordon's expression, but it didn't change. "They have the ranch up the road."

"Do you raise cattle?" Gordon asked.

"Steve raises and trains horses. Most of the rest of the land is leased to these guys. I bought the ranch as more of a getaway and found that I really liked it here," Wilson said, and Mario saw him smile proudly at Steve.

"Steve's amazing with horses," Dakota said. "We send him the ones that we have difficulty training, and he works miracles." Dakota set a bowl of pasta with sauce on the table, and Wally added a plate of garlic bread and a bowl of salad. "Who wants a beer?" Dakota asked as he passed bottles to everyone without waiting for an answer. He and Wally then sat down, and everyone began to eat.

"I was in the diner a few days ago," Steve said as he took some salad. "I overheard some of the older men talking about your dad. Everyone still misses him."

"So do we," Wally said softly, taking Dakota's hand. Mario saw Gordon look around the table quizzically. "Dakota's dad died about two years ago," Wally explained. "He had multiple sclerosis and was bedridden at the end, but you'd have to look far and wide to find a better person. He hounded Dakota to go back to medical school, putting his own care in the hands of me and nurses so he could see Dakota become a doctor."

"And he had quite a past," Haven said as he filled his plate with spaghetti. "He and my mother fell in love, and he tried to protect her from my abusive father."

"Was his room the one with the big window that overlooks the paddock?" Gordon asked. "I saw it from outside."

"That was his. We put it in so he could watch the hands work with the horses," Dakota said. "Anyway, I was telling Mario that we're going to have the barbeque this summer. We stopped for a while, but it's time, and Dad would kill me if he knew we'd stopped. He loved a party." Dakota filled his plate and began to eat. The conversation continued around the table. Mario kept glancing at Gordon, who seemed to be taking in everyone's stories. Mario told Wally and Dakota about the deputy's visit.

"We also got Wally's enclosure done," Gordon said with a smile. "When are the animals coming?"

"In a few days," Wally said.

Everyone ate until they couldn't eat another bite. Of course, about that time, Wally brought out a cake he'd gotten from the small bakery in town. He cut it and passed pieces to everyone, who all seemed to find room anyway.

Once the food had been eaten and the cake devoured, everyone moved into the living room and settled in for the evening. Mario loved times like this. He sat on the sofa next to Gordon and spent a few hours laughing, joking, and telling stories, until by mutual unspoken agreement, it was time to head to bed.

Mario said his good-nights, and Gordon did as well before the two of them walked across the yard. "Wally and Dakota have great friends."

"Yes, they do," Mario agreed, and Gordon paused.

"What I don't understand is why Dakota and Wally own the ranch, and Haven and Phillip have the ranch next door, but Haven seems to manage everything. It's confusing."

"I guess it looks that way. Actually, Dakota, Wally, Haven, and Phillip all own the ranch corporation. It's complicated and I'm not privy to the details, but they merged the ranches years ago, and Haven manages the day-to-day cattle operation while Dakota and Wally handle the business side. That frees Wally to grow his veterinary practice and allowed Dakota to go to medical school and build his practice here. Haven's ranch was smaller than Dakota's, so most of the hands are centered here, and I'm the foreman reporting to Haven over everything, but Haven tends to take care of things around where he lives and I handle things here."

"So it's Haven that runs things?" Gordon asked.

"Generally, yes, but when it comes to the care of the animals, Wally is the undisputed king. Each of the four of them has skills they bring to the table. Phillip is an accountant by trade, so he keeps the records, Haven manages the cattle, Wally manages the health records, and everyone reports to Dakota, who acts as a sort of CEO,

I guess. Among them, they're an unbeatable team, and the ranch prospers because of it. There's no place I'd rather live and work than right here." Mario reached over to Gordon and took his hand. "I think this place may turn out to be good for you too."

Gordon looked down at their entwined hands; then Mario felt a slight squeeze. He was about to lead Gordon toward the house when he felt a slight tug. Gordon led him around the barn to one of the paddocks. A colt just a few months old ran around while his mother alternately watched and ate her hay. "I love watching them," Gordon said as the colt walked over to them and leaned on the fencing. Gordon reached out and lightly patted the colt's neck. The colt moved closer, nuzzling along Gordon's chest, probably looking for treats. "They're so innocent, with no guile, and you don't have to wonder what's going on behind their eyes."

Mario nodded but remained quiet.

"I spent so many years meeting people who smiled and laughed to your face, and as soon as you turned your back, they were pulling out machine guns or strapping bombs to themselves." Gordon continued stroking the colt's neck. "This little guy will never know anything like that, and I wish I didn't."

"Are you still having the dreams?" Mario asked, and Gordon nodded.

"They said I'd probably always have them. Lots of guys do. They used to scare the life out of me because I really thought I was back there. Now at least I know they're only dreams." Gordon continued stroking the colt, and Mario kept an eye on the mother. "But some of them are so real I can feel the sand in my shorts." Gordon stepped back from the colt, and he bounded back to his mother, who nuzzled him before returning to her feed. They watched the horses for a few more minutes, and then Gordon turned and began walking to the foreman's house. Mario followed, and once inside, he wondered what Gordon had in mind. Gordon didn't seem to be in a talkative mood. He expected Gordon to head to his room and go to bed, but instead he slid his now work-roughened hand into Mario's and led him down the hall.

To Mario's slight surprise, Gordon opened the door to Mario's bedroom and led him inside. "Are you sure about this?" Mario asked. "Because if you're not, we don't have to do this. Earlier you were worried about…."

Gordon placed a finger over Mario's lips. "Sometimes you talk too damn much," Gordon said. He removed his finger and stepped closer, tugging Mario to him. He pressed their chests together, Gordon's heat radiating through their clothes. Mario was about to respond to Gordon's teasing when the words were sucked away by a kiss that short-circuited Mario's brain. Gordon pressed him further into the room, and Mario took small steps backward until he reached the bed. Gordon continued pressing him back, then cradled him onto the bed.

Mario entwined his arms around Gordon's neck, intensifying the kiss and receiving even more intensity in response. Gordon's tongue took command of his mouth, and whenever Mario tried to take back some control, Gordon fought harder. Mario nipped at Gordon's lower lip, earning a deep growl and a kiss that made Mario's eyes roll to the back of his head.

Gordon pressed Mario's head against the mattress with a deep, penetrating kiss after kiss. Gordon gently unwound Mario's arms from around his neck and took both his hands in one of his huge ones before stretching Mario's arms over his head and holding them there.

Mario was used to being in charge in the bedroom, so giving control to someone else felt a bit strange, but the sheer power of Gordon's control was more than he could fight, so it was either put an end to things or go with what Gordon wanted. When he felt Gordon pull his shirt up and stroke his skin, Mario arched his back, still trying to figure how to take back control. However, once Gordon plucked a nipple with his thumb like he was playing an instrument, thoughts of anything other than what Gordon was doing to him flew from his mind and he gave himself over.

Mario heard fabric tear and then his T-shirt fell away from his body. Gordon mumbled something that sounded like "sorry" but then Gordon backed away and tugged off his own shirt before taking possession of Mario's mouth once again as their chests met skin to skin. Mario moaned softly, and Gordon scooted them both further onto the bed. Gordon gentled their kiss, tugging on Mario's lower lip until it popped away from Gordon's.

Mario held his breath, wondering what Gordon was going to do next. He found out when Gordon ran his tongue down Mario's neck and along his shoulder before nipping lightly at the sensitive spot at the base of Mario's neck. "What...?" Mario asked, and Gordon shushed him almost instantly.

"Don't talk, feel," Gordon told him before tilting his head and clamping his lips around Mario's right nipple. Gordon sucked and nibbled on the sensitive skin. At first, Mario tried to get away, the sensations nearly overwhelming, but Gordon wouldn't let him, and as the sensation built and built, Mario squirmed and moaned. Arching his back, Mario pressed his chest against Gordon's face and wrapped his arms around Gordon's waist, tugging him closer. Mario let his head loll back as he shivered with excitement. "See? Just feel," Gordon said, sliding his hands down Mario's back and under the waistband of his jeans.

Mario wasn't sure how he felt about where Gordon's hands were going, but he let them slip into his jeans, Gordon's big hands each cupping a butt cheek, holding him to Gordon's warmth. Mario splayed himself on the bed, letting Gordon play his body like a violin. He'd gotten so used to being in control that he hadn't realized just how amazing it could feel to let someone else see to his pleasure, and Gordon sure as hell knew what he was doing.

Gordon pulled his hands out of Mario's pants, opened his belt, and popped the buttons on his jeans. Mario felt the bed shift as

Gordon climbed off. Before he could ask what was happening, Gordon pulled off his shoes, letting them thunk onto the floor before yanking down his jeans and underwear and pulling them off his legs, leaving him naked, dick hard and throbbing. Mario expected Gordon to climb back on the bed, but Gordon was full of surprises.

Mario watched, his mouth watering, as Gordon unfastened his belt. Mario longed to touch, and sat up, but Gordon pushed him lightly back onto the mattress. Mario jumped slightly when Gordon touched his ankles, his surprise turning to leg-shaking excitement as Gordon slowly ran his hands up Mario's calves and thighs before skimming over his hips and up his chest. Mario tried to catch his breath, only able to gasp as Gordon lowered his body on top of Mario's, and instantly he was breathless again. The skin-to-skin contact made Mario's head swim, and he breathed deeply just before Gordon took him in a deep, probing kiss.

"God," Mario hissed without thinking as he thrust his hips forward, sliding his dick along Gordon's hip, creating the most glorious friction.

The kiss stopped and Gordon stared into Mario's eyes. He appeared to be looking for something, and then he slowly slithered down Mario's body. Mario arched his back as Gordon sucked his nipples again, swirling his tongue around his chest before kissing and nibbling his way down Mario's stomach.

Mario didn't dare move as his breath caught in glorious anticipation. He closed his eyes and prayed silently to all the gods he could think of. Then he felt Gordon's lips on his cock, encircling him. With agonizing slowness, Gordon sucked him deeper. Mario thrust forward, and Gordon placed a hand on his hip to still his movement before taking him deep and hard. For the millionth time, Mario tried to catch his breath and failed.

Mario lifted his hands off the bed and lightly placed them on Gordon's head, cradling it as his short hair lightly pricked his palms. "You feel so good," Mario whispered, but Gordon made no noise, only sucking harder. Mario groaned as he began to shake with barely controlled excitement. "Fuck, Gord!" Mario cried, throwing his head back. He'd tried being quiet, but couldn't stand it any longer. "You're going to kill me."

Gordon chuckled and lifted his head. Mario slipped from between his lips, his cock slapping lightly against his stomach. "You seem to want to talk a lot," Gordon teased.

"It is okay to talk during sex, you know," Mario teased back. "In fact, it's okay to scream."

Gordon crawled up Mario's body, positioning his lips just above Mario's. "If it's screaming you want, I'll make you scream yourself hoarse," Gordon said softly but with enough power behind his words to make Mario shiver in the warm room. "Is that what you want?"

Mario nodded slowly, his mouth hanging open. No one had ever manipulated him the way Gordon could. Like Gordon knew where each of Mario's buttons was located and the exact order to push them in. "Yes," Mario gasped before swallowing hard. Gordon seemed full of surprises as he climbed off the bed and stood up, extending his hand. Mario took it, and Gordon led him from the bedroom to the bathroom.

Gordon started the shower and waited for the water to warm before stepping inside and tugging Mario after him. It seemed the quiet Gordon was back, and once he stood under the water, Mario waited. Gordon rubbed the bar of soap between his huge hands and began soaping Mario's skin. Slowly and carefully, every inch of his front was washed and caressed. Mario rinsed off the soap, and Gordon turned him around, pressing him against the tile, with his chest to Mario's back. Gordon washed his back and then slid lower, soaping his butt, while he ghosted his fingers over Mario's hole. "Spread your legs," Gordon told him, and Mario groaned as he complied.

Gordon washed the backs of his legs, teasing his way up Mario's inner thighs until Mario's legs shook and he could barely stand. "Does that feel good?" Gordon asked as he slid his hands between Mario's legs, gliding soapy fingers under his balls and then up along his aching shaft. Mario shivered and snapped his hips slightly. Gordon then pulled his hand back and spread Mario's cheeks, running his hand along the cleft. Mario wasn't used to being touched there, but Gordon had him thrusting back into the light touch, searching for more. Gordon settled his fingers at Mario's opening, lightly teasing the flesh while he leaned close, pressing his chest to Mario's back before sucking his ear.

Mario moaned wantonly, pressing his hips back. Gordon's touch was so light, so gentle, it almost wasn't there, and he wanted, no, *needed*, more. Suddenly, Gordon was gone, and all sensation ceased. Mario turned to look over his shoulder and moved away from the wall. Gordon soaped his own chest and then gathered Mario into his huge arms and guided him under the spray. Their chests slid against each other, and Mario closed his eyes, wantonly enjoying being held.

The cooling spray washed away the soap, and Gordon turned off the water. Stepping out of the shower, he handed Mario a towel before grabbing his own. They dried themselves and then hung up the towels. Then Gordon led him into the bedroom. "Lay on your belly," Gordon said, and Mario spread out on the bed and waited. He felt Gordon climb on the bed and settle between his legs. He stroked up Mario's legs, and Mario sighed and tensed, wondering just what he was in for. Mario half expected him to go for his butt, but instead Gordon continued up his back, deeply massaging his muscles. "I thought you needed to relax," Gordon said, and he used his magic fingers to work into every muscle of Mario's back.

Mario closed his eyes and relished the intimate touch. He felt Gordon hover over him. "God, you're good," Mario moaned softly.

Gordon whispered something Mario couldn't quite catch and slid his hands to Mario's butt. He massaged Mario's cheeks, touching gently. Mario almost missed the fact that, over time, the massage became more and more intimate. Gordon lightly tugged apart his cheeks, skimming his fingers deeper and deeper into Mario's cleft, yet not quite touching his opening before moving away. Again and again, Gordon worked his skin, teasing him but not quite going for the gold.

Mario arched his back and nearly growled like one of Wally's cats when Gordon teased him again. He could hardly stand it and so very much wanted Gordon to touch him. Then Gordon moved away altogether. Mario whimpered at the loss and then started when he felt a searing wetness against his skin. Gordon was licking him, swirling his tongue on his skin.

Gordon tugged up Mario's hips, parting his cheeks in the process. Mario whined softly when Gordon's tongue skimmed over the skin of his opening. Then, like one of his kisses, Gordon intensified the sensation, nibbling the skin of Mario's opening before probing deep and hard. "Jesus Christ!" Mario cried, throwing his head back as Gordon rimmed him half to death. Mario throbbed with unbelievable desire as Gordon kept up his assault on his skin. For the first time, Mario also heard Gordon moan softly, and that inflamed him even more.

One of Gordon's fingers joined his tongue, and Mario's eyes crossed as Gordon slowly pressed a finger inside his body, still nipping at his skin with his lips. Mario began to wonder if he was going to burst into tears, the sensations were so nearly overwhelming. Gordon inserted a second finger to join the first and the stretch burn added to everything else.

Slowly, Gordon removed his fingers and lowered Mario's hips back to the bed. Without thinking, Mario rolled onto his back, and Gordon lifted his legs, pressing Mario's knees to his chest. Then Mario wondered if there were any condoms. He hadn't been with anyone since David left, and he hadn't needed to think about supplies. Gordon leaned over him, and he heard the nightstand drawer open. Gordon grunted softly and rummaged around. Then he found what he was looking for and tore open the package. Gordon fumbled with the condom for a second, and then Mario felt Gordon's slicked cock press to his opening.

Gordon leaned over him, kissing Mario deep and hard as he slowly pressed forward, entering Mario's body. The stretch and bloom of exquisite pain made Mario quiver. Gordon paused, and Mario wrapped his arms around Gordon's neck, kissing him hard enough that he thought he might have tasted blood. It wasn't until he felt Gordon deep inside him that Mario felt he could breathe again. "Relax and feel," Gordon said, and he slowly rocked his hips. "Just let yourself relish the sensation." Mario nodded and closed his eyes, doing what Gordon said. "Watch me," Gordon told him, stroking his cheek. "Watching is part of the sensation. Don't close off any part of yourself."

Mario breathed deeply as wave after wave of sensation originated from where Gordon pegged the spot inside him repeatedly. He watched Gordon's body as a light sheen of sweat broke out on his skin, making him glisten in the low light. Gordon stroked Mario's chest, snapping his hips faster, sending vibrations of pleasure through Mario's entire body. Not quite sure what to do with his hands, Mario gripped the bedding in his fists and held on for dear life.

"That's it, give yourself over to me and let yourself feel everything."

"I am," Mario gasped.

Gordon wrapped a hand around Mario's cock and stroked him slowly and firmly. Mario thrust lightly into the touch, and Gordon drove deep into his body. Mario was overwhelmed, every cell in his body screaming for release. Mario heard sound echo off the walls of the room and realized he had made that sound.

Mario was no longer in control of his own body. Gordon had driven him to the point where all he could do was breathe and let the pleasure wash over him.

"That's it, let it all go," Gordon whispered, stroking him harder and faster.

Mario had never felt anything like this, his body and pleasure completely in the hands of someone else. He pulled at the bedding as his release bloomed at the base of his spine and slowly spread. His back tingled, and then his legs and arms. Once the sensation reached his head, Mario clamped his eyes closed and screamed at the top of his lungs as he came, shaking, with lights dancing behind his eyes.

Breathing slowly in and out, eyes still closed, Mario floated. Gordon had stilled, but their bodies were connected. Mario felt Gordon stroking his skin. "Wow," Mario whispered softly as he slowly sank back to the present and opened his eyes. Gordon gazed down at him with a small smile on his face. "You said I'd scream," Mario said, and Gordon nodded, his eyes shining. They both gasped softly as their bodies separated. Mario lowered his legs, feeling a bit like a wrung-out rag doll, his eyes drifting closed once again. The bed shook as Gordon climbed off, and Mario heard him leave the room and then return. Mario felt a warm cloth clean his skin, but he could barely open his eyes. Gordon chuckled softly, and after blotting Mario with a towel, he left the room once again.

When he didn't return, Mario opened his eyes, looking toward the doorway. Gordon stood, leaning against the frame. "I wasn't sure what you'd want me to do," Gordon said, and Mario moved to the side of the bed, pulling back the covers as an invitation. Gordon slowly moved forward, turning out the light before climbing beneath the covers. "I've never slept with someone like this before," Gordon whispered through the darkness.

"You never stayed with anyone after sex before?" Mario asked, shifting to get comfortable.

"Never had the chance before. 'Don't ask, don't tell' left a lot of us with very few choices, and I always had to be careful, so sex was usually fast and very quiet unless you could find a private place to be alone. And even then, it was usually quick because I had to get back," Gordon explained. "So, no, I don't really know what's expected."

Mario rested his head on Gordon's shoulder. "What's expected is what you're comfortable with and what makes you happy," Mario said before turning to kiss Gordon's skin. He slowly stroked Gordon's chest, making lazy circles on his skin. "Go to sleep. There's nothing you need to worry about."

"What if I dream?"

"I'll be right here, and nothing will happen to you," Mario promised, closing his eyes. He slowed his stroking and then stopped, resting his hand as the activity from the day caught up with him. Mario couldn't stop exhaustion as it crept up on him. "Go to sleep," he whispered, holding Gordon a little tighter.

Chapter Five

SOMETHING wasn't right. Gordon sat up and looked around. The men from his unit were asleep around him in the barracks. Stacks was sleeping on one side and Bottles on the other, like they should be. Gordon rolled over and felt the bedding against his skin along with the usual bits of sand he could never seem to get rid of. All was quiet, or as quiet as possible with a dozen sleeping men, half of them snoring to some degree. That was the first thing he'd learned—to sleep through anything and in any position. All the men were in their bunks like they should be. There was no shelling or sounds coming from outside. Everything was as it should be as far as he could tell. Gordon lay back down on his bunk, wondering what had woken him. A breeze wafted through the room, cool and fresh. That had to be it. The air was too comfortable, too cool. Getting up, Gordon moved silently past the sleeping men, seeking the source of the fresh air, something he hadn't felt in months. At the door to the room, he turned the knob and slowly pulled it open. Fresh, cool air wafted in even as he saw the usual sight of more barracks, desert, and sand, endless sand. And yet the breeze continued.

A sharp sound broke the night, and Gordon hit the floor, looking around to see where the shot had come from. "Gordon, it's me," a voice from outside told him. "Open your eyes. It's Mario." Gordon did as he was told, and the barracks dissolved into a bedroom in a real house, and he wasn't on the barracks floor, but lying flat on a rug. "It's okay. You were dreaming. Let me help you up." Mario took his arm, and Gordon stood up on unsteady legs.

"Is everything okay?" Gordon asked as he looked around him. Everything looked normal, but the feeling of uneasiness he'd had from the dream lingered. "Something isn't right."

"You were dreaming. Everything is fine," Mario said, but Gordon pulled his arm away.

"No, it's not. Something is wrong." Gordon hurried to his room, yanked on a pair of pants, and pulled on a shirt before shoving his feet into a pair of shoes. "Get dressed," he ordered Mario as he headed for the door.

He stepped into the night, the cool air surrounding him in the near silence. That was what was wrong. It was too quiet. It almost seemed like someone or something had shut off the usual night chorus. Then he heard them—voices on the breeze that shouldn't be there. Gordon raced back to his room and pulled out the steel box from under his bed. He opened it and pulled out the Luger, seated the clip, and then headed back outside. The feeling of wrongness was still there.

"What is it?" Mario asked.

"Call the sheriff and get everyone up. Turn on every light you can find and stay indoors," Gordon whispered urgently and then headed into the darkness.

He stuck to the shadows and quickly reached the ranch house, slowly turned the corner in near darkness. He wished he had night-vision goggles, but followed his hearing for the slightest sound out of place. The soft clang of metal told him exactly where they were. Rounding the corner, he looked toward the enclosures as lights came on in the ranch house. Then lights outside came on. Just enough light reached the enclosures for Gordon to see two men standing still near the one they'd just built. "These are empty," he heard someone swear.

Gordon lifted his gun and shot into the air. "Stay where you are. I can drop all of you where you stand," Gordon growled, and the two figures went as still as statues. "Move slowly into the light and keep your hands visible." The two figures slowly moved closer, becoming easier to see in the glow of the lights from the house. Gordon moved toward them, his gun at the ready, stance braced to shoot at any second, all of his training kicking in. Sirens sounded, and he saw the two men look at each other. "Don't even think of moving," Gordon barked.

"What's going on?" Wally asked from behind him.

Gordon didn't turn around. "Stay inside and away from the doors and windows. I have things under control."

The sirens got closer and louder. Gordon didn't take his eyes off either of the men. "Lie down on the ground and don't move a muscle."

"Okay, man," a shaky voice said, and slowly the two men went first to their knees and then lay on the ground.

"They're out there," Gordon heard Wally say and turned his head slightly.

"Two men. I have them lying on the grass. I don't know if they're armed," Gordon said without lowering his gun.

"We can take it from here," one of the deputies said, and Gordon slowly lowered his weapon. The deputies pulled theirs, and Gordon stepped back and away slowly. Gordon knew the officers would be nervous about anyone with a gun, so he placed it on the ground and stood off to the side without moving. He watched as the deputies reached the two men, cuffed them, and then hauled them to their feet.

"Hey, we were just doing what was right. These people are abusing these animals," one of the men protested as they were led around the house. "Set them free!" His choice of words sounded very familiar. Once they were gone, Wally came out of the house, carrying a flashlight, and rushed across the grass to the enclosures. Gordon picked up his gun and took it into the house, removing the clip and setting both on the table before taking a seat to wait for the deputies.

Wally came back in the house looking relieved. "All the cats are fine. They must not have gotten to the enclosures that contained the animals. All the gates of the empty enclosure had been pulled open. Thank God they came today or we'd have had a mess." Wally sat down at the table, staring at Gordon's gun. "You didn't shoot any of them, did you?"

"No. I shot into the air to scare them," Gordon said.

A knock sounded on the front door, and Wally got up to answer it, returning a few minutes later with one of the deputies. "Were you the man with the gun?" he asked Gordon, and Gordon nodded, pulling out his wallet to show him his permit.

"I fired once in the air to scare them," Gordon explained without reaching for the gun. He let the deputy examine the weapon as well as the clip to satisfy himself that only one shot had been fired. "I didn't shoot at them, but I would have if they made a move toward me or one of the animals." Gordon looked to Wally, who explained what he'd found out back.

"You have got to get these people," Wally said. "If they'd let these animals free, you'd have to hunt them down and would have no choice but to shoot them. In the cages, they're safe, but loose they're a danger, and these people seem intent on letting them loose."

"Maybe you shouldn't have them," the deputy challenged, and Wally jumped to his feet, standing toe to toe with the much larger deputy.

"Maybe if you were able to do your job and catch these people, there wouldn't be an issue. So I suggest you keep your opinions to yourself. I am fully licensed by the state and I'm a veterinarian. I believe that makes my opinion much more accurate than yours." Wally didn't move when the deputy puffed out his chest. "And you better believe that my first call in the morning is going to be to the sheriff, and the next will be to the head of the town council. Now, I assume you've talked to the people who trespassed onto our ranch?" Wally's eyes blazed, and it wasn't until Dakota touched his shoulder that he backed away from the deputy.

The deputy swallowed hard. "We haven't yet, but we will at the station."

"Then unless there's something you need from us, I suggest you get to it," Wally said. The deputy consulted his notes, asked a few basic questions about each of them, and then left the room. "Jerk!" Wally yelled once the front door closed. "Stupid, arrogant asshole!" he added vehemently.

"Wally, hon, it's okay. We'll make calls in the morning," Dakota said. "Are the cats okay?"

"Yes. They were upset and prowling in their cages, but they'll settle down and be fine," Wally answered as Dakota pulled him into his arms.

"Everything will be fine," Dakota said reassuringly before turning to Mario. "Tomorrow, I want to figure out how we're going to run electricity out to the cages, and then we'll install motion-sensor lights that point away from the cages. If anyone gets close again, it'll turn on the lights and we'll all know. We probably should have done this a while ago, but we definitely need to do it now, for all our sakes." Dakota held Wally close to him, whispering into his ear. Gordon saw Wally nod, and the two of them left the room.

"We should get to bed as well," Mario said, and Gordon yawned. Getting up, he took the gun and clip from the table. Mario turned out the lights, and they left by the front door. The lights in the rest of the house switched out as they walked across the yard. By the time they reached the foreman's house, the ranch was quiet and largely dark.

"You were amazing," Mario said once they were in the bedroom with the door closed. Mario pulled off his shirt and dropped his pants before getting into bed. "You knew exactly what to do."

Gordon stripped as well and joined Mario in bed, pulling him to his body, kissing Mario hard. His blood raced with excitement, and Gordon rolled them on the bed, pressing Mario into the mattress. "I need...," Gordon said softly. "Everything around me feels like it's slipping away and I'm back in the desert." He wasn't sure how to explain the feelings that threatened to overwhelm him. When he'd been holding his gun, he'd snapped fully into Marine mode, and he wasn't quite sure how to get back again.

Mario met his kiss with one of his own, hard and demanding. "Then take," Mario answered, and soon the room filled with the sounds of urgent, nearly unstoppable need.

GORDON spent much of the next day running electrical wiring out to the cat enclosures. He, Mario, and Wally decided where all the lights would go, and since he had electrical experience, Gordon was elected to complete the wiring. "Mario said I should come out here and see if you needed help," one of the hands said as he approached where Gordon was working.

"Sure, Paul," Gordon said, and he watched the young man's face, relieved he'd remembered his name correctly. "I have the wiring laid. You can help me drill the holes into the posts for the wiring, and then we'll need to run the wire through them. Then we can place them in the ground and set them in concrete."

"Okay," Paul said with enthusiasm and got the drill.

"I marked where each hole will need to go. Drill the hole, and we'll thread the wire before using the plastic caps to seal it and make the hole watertight," Gordon explained, and Paul went to work. Paul drilled the holes and Gordon finished running the wire.

"Is it true you were a Marine?" Paul asked as he threaded the wire through the first post.

"I was in the Corps, yes," Gordon answered, stopping what he was doing, "but once a Marine, always a Marine."

"That tough, huh?" Paul asked.

"More like life-changing. The process of becoming one of the best in the world gets into every part of you," Gordon explained, but it was tough to make people who hadn't been through what he had understand what it meant to be a Marine. Gordon had been one of the best in the world and he was proud of it, but the end had tainted everything, even the best of times.

"I thought of joining the Marines, but I didn't want to go back into the closet.... Was that hard for you?" Paul asked.

"Sometimes," Gordon answered, continuing with his work. He rarely talked about things like that with anyone, so he hoped Paul would change the subject.

"I have this one done," Paul announced, and Gordon checked over his work before placing the pole in the ground. Paul filled the hole with quick-set cement and then thoroughly doused it with water. Once the water drained away, they topped off the hole with dirt, and Paul moved on to the next pole. Gordon went back to what he was doing, and thankfully the conversation dropped off for a while.

"Looks good," Wally told them as he came up to the enclosure. "How long will it take?"

"The wiring should be in place today, and tomorrow I'll shut off the power and add the connection to the breaker box," Gordon said. Wally motioned with his head toward the house. "Keep working, and I'll be right back," Gordon told Paul and followed Wally.

"After my call this morning I was starved, so I stopped in the diner in town. I sat at the counter and saw two people come in. They were wearing uniforms, shirts buttoned up to their necks, I'm sure you know the type," Wally said, and Gordon nodded, swallowing hard. He knew exactly the type. "I wasn't trying to eavesdrop, but they sat next to me and it sounded like they were looking for someone. A Marine. They didn't talk about why they were looking for this person, and I didn't volunteer anything, but are they looking for you?"

Gordon took a deep breath and sighed. "I think they might be, but I've done nothing wrong. A friend of mine called a while ago and said they'd contacted him to see if he knew where I was. He didn't, thankfully."

"They seemed to believe the person they were looking for was in the area, and they didn't ask questions or say a name, but I sort of figured there couldn't be too many Marines, or ex-Marines, around here." Wally paused. "Why would they be looking for you?"

"I don't know. But when the sphincters in the dress uniforms are looking for you, it isn't good. They tried to get my friend to reenlist. I've sort of hoped they wouldn't be able to find me because I've been off the grid for so long."

"You realize that sheriff and police records are computerized, and the last few encounters you've had with the sheriff will give them your location if they check with them? That's probably why they're here in town. That is, if it's you they're looking for," Wally explained.

Gordon sighed softly. "I should get back to work."

Wally nodded, and Gordon returned to the electrical work, but his mind stayed on what Wally had said.

"Is this okay?" Paul asked, showing him the post.

"Yes. That looks fine," Gordon said, and they set the post in the ground. By the time that post was done and set, the heat of the day was on them full force. Gordon pulled off his T-shirt and shoved the tail of it in his back pocket before returning to work. The breeze, what little there was of it, felt good on his skin, but after a while, sweat ran down his skin in tiny rivers. A few times Gordon caught Paul looking, but he ignored it and continued working.

"You know," Paul said from behind him, and Gordon paused where he was making the final connections to the light at the top of the first pole. "I was wondering if you might like to go into town for a drink sometime." Gordon turned at the top of the ladder, seeing Paul rub the back of his neck nervously. Gordon descended the ladder and leaned against it.

"That would be real nice, Paul," he began, searching for the words that wouldn't hurt him. He rarely went into town, and other than an occasional beer, he didn't drink much. Alcohol tended to dull the senses, and that was something Gordon wasn't too interested in. "I'd like to have a beer with a friend."

He saw some of the excitement fade from Paul's expression. Gordon wasn't sure what was going on between him and Mario, and Paul seemed like a nice kid. "Sure," Paul said, clearly disappointed.

"Paul, you can never have enough friends," Gordon said, his heart suddenly aching for the friends he'd lost. Gordon flashed a smile he knew probably looked a bit fake before turning around to climb the ladder again. He didn't want Paul or anyone to see the aching pain on his face. He knew his friends were gone, and he knew it was his fault, but....

"Did you have friends in the Corps?" Paul asked a bit tentatively, interrupting Gordon's thoughts.

"Yes," he answered as he schooled his expression. "But you think of them as family, closer than brothers."

"Did you lose friends?" Paul asked, and Gordon nodded.

"Everyone lost friends at one point or another," Gordon explained before returning to his work, hoping Paul would let the subject drop. The loss he carried and sometimes thought he had control over seemed way too close to the surface. Gordon finished wiring the lamp and secured it to the post. However, instead of descending the ladder, he stayed where he was, watching. The landscape around him was so different from Iraq, but in his mind, they morphed together—the heat, sweat, Paul talking behind him—and suddenly everything changed.

Gordon nearly fell off the ladder at what he momentarily thought was gunfire. Pulling himself back to the present, he stumbled down the ladder to the ground. "Sorry," Paul said. "I banged two of the poles together. I didn't mean to startle you."

"It's okay," Gordon said, walking to the cooler, where he got a bottle of water, downing the entire thing in a few gulps. He had to do something to clear his head. Once he was done, he handed one to Paul. "You need to hydrate in this heat." Paul didn't say anything, but he took the bottle and drank the water, watching Gordon like he was about to do something crazy. "Sometimes the memories take over."

"Like post-traumatic stress?" Paul asked, and Gordon nodded. "It's cool." Paul finished drinking the bottle of water and went back to work. Gordon did the same, but noticed that Paul spent the next hour working gingerly without making any unnecessary noise.

"I'm not going to go off," Gordon said and turned around to Paul. "It's just that sometimes a sound or scent will transport me back. Unfortunately, it's usually to the bad stuff. But I'm not going to attack you or think you're a suicide bomber or something." Paul nodded and seemed to work more normally after that.

By the end of the day, all the wiring was in place, the poles with their lights attached set in concrete. "Tomorrow we'll hook everything up to the power and test it out before burying the cables," Gordon said as he and Paul looked over their handiwork. "You did great. Thanks." Gordon lightly clapped Paul on the shoulder, and he grinned before checking his watch.

"Thanks. I'll help you clean up and then I gotta go," Paul said.

"I'll take care of things here. No problem," Gordon offered.

"Thanks," Paul said, already hurrying away. "I'll see you tomorrow," Paul called, and Gordon nodded.

Gordon gathered up the wire, making sure it was rolled properly before placing all the tools in the box and gathering up the bits of plastic packaging that seemed to get everywhere no matter how careful they were to try to keep them together.

"How's it going?" Mario asked as he approached. "Did Paul work out?"

"He was great. Good worker. Talked a bit, though," Gordon said, and Mario smiled.

"He'll talk your ear off if you let him. But he's a good kid." Mario studied him for a few seconds, tilting his head slightly. "What?"

"Paul asked me for a drink," Gordon said and Mario instantly stepped closer.

"What did you tell him?" Mario asked with the slightest hint of a growl.

"That it would be nice to have a drink with a friend," Gordon answered innocently, trying not to smile at Mario's jealousy. He wasn't willing to say he already had someone else in his life because he had no idea what was going on between him and Mario. He liked being around him, spending time with him, and the sex was explosively amazing. But he still figured Mario was hung up on his ex, and Gordon, well, there were just too many things about himself that he wasn't sure of.

"I'm glad," Mario told him, moving closer, and Gordon felt himself stiffen. "What happened?"

"I had one of those…." Gordon hesitated. "Dreams, for lack of a better term, but I was wide awake. That hasn't happened in a long time. I think it's because Wally told me he saw Navy people in town and he thought they might be trying to find me."

"Why? Have you done something wrong?" Mario asked.

Gordon wanted to say he hadn't, but the words wouldn't come. "I don't know. Maybe. I can't remember." Gordon took a deep breath.

"Hey, it's okay," Mario said as he took Gordon's hand.

"No, it's not," Gordon said. "I can't remember anything, and my best friends died. I know it has to be my fault." Gordon turned away, slipping his hand from Mario's. He lifted the roll of wire and slid it over his arm, then began picking up the rest of the supplies. Once he had everything he could carry, Gordon strode around the side of the house toward the equipment shed. He put everything away and returned to pack up the tools. To his relief, Mario wasn't waiting for him, and he finished cleaning up, carrying the tools to the equipment shed as well. He wasn't interesting in talking about it.

Once he'd put everything away, Gordon shuffled toward the foremen's house, intending to clean up and spend the rest of the day in his room. Instead, he found Mario in the living room, waiting in ambush. "We need to talk," Mario said, and Gordon rolled his eyes, continuing into his bedroom and then closing the door with emphasis. He half expected Mario to come banging on his door, but Gordon heard nothing. After getting undressed, he gathered clean clothes and walked across the hall to the bathroom to clean up.

Gordon set his clothes on the counter and started the water, stepping under the spray once the water had warmed. He sighed and let the hot water wash away some of the tension and strain. He wished it would wash away the fear as well, but that always seemed to stay with him.

The shower curtain moved, and Gordon tensed, nearly lunging at the intruder until he saw Mario step into the shower. Gordon growled loud and deep in his throat before grabbing Mario and pressing him to the tile with his body. He crashed his mouth to

Mario's, and Gordon heard Mario whimper, but he didn't let up as he took complete control. Grinding his hips against Mario's, Gordon rutted like an animal, feeling Mario moving against him. He needed, and instinct took over everything.

"Gordon," Mario snapped, pushing on his shoulders.

He stopped, wondering if he'd hurt Mario, but then Mario kissed him, and Gordon took control once again. They didn't talk any more, the bathroom and shower filling with grunts and throaty moans. Gordon felt Mario shake in his arms, crying out into his mouth as he came between them. Gordon pressed Mario hard against the tile, thrusting his hips until his release began to build. Mario pressed against him, hard. Gordon stepped back, and Mario quickly sank to his knees, swallowing him deep and fast. Gordon thrust his hips, clamping his eyes closed as his climax built and built, encouraged by Mario's hot, magic mouth. When he could control himself no longer, Gordon lifted his head and howled toward the ceiling as he came, quivering from head to toe.

Gordon nearly collapsed onto the floor of the shower, but managed to steady himself using the wall. Breathing deeply, he felt Mario's lips move away from him. Seconds later, Gordon was being held and maneuvered beneath the running water. "Just relax and let it go."

Gordon wanted to ask Mario what he meant, but didn't have the energy. The water poured over his head and down his body. Then Mario washed him, soapy hands wandering all over him. His back, chest, legs, arms, butt, and hair were washed. Gordon stood almost still and let Mario do what he wanted. After a final rinse, Mario turned the water off and Gordon followed him out of the shower. Gordon dried himself on autopilot and then dressed in the clothes he'd brought to the bathroom with him.

Still feeling like his brain had been sucked away, Gordon padded, barefoot, to the living room, and Mario joined him a few minutes later, sitting next to him on the sofa. "I know you don't want to talk about what happened, but I think you might need to."

"That's just it—I don't remember," Gordon snapped.

"Then tell me what you do remember," Mario said. "Maybe that will remove the block you're feeling."

"What if it's all my fault?" Gordon asked.

"Have you ever backed away from responsibility for your actions? You didn't with Wally and Dakota when you were duped into trying to set Wally's cats free. You owned up to that, so why can't you own up to this? Good or bad, you need to try to remember what happened."

Gordon shook his head even as he began to talk. "My platoon was on patrol. We were supposed to help secure a region of Fallujah that had seen an increase in enemy activity. The thing was, things had died down. We'd already taken out some large terrorist-type cells and the entire area was safer. I remember people out in the market we were patrolling selling fruit, vegetables, all kinds of household items. Women completely covered, accompanied by men chaperoning them as they did the shopping. The sellers even tried to get us to buy things. But of course we weren't allowed; we were on duty. The atmosphere was almost festive, even if it was hot as hell." Gordon could almost hear the cacophony of voices, dogs, camels, and hawkers all overlying and entwining with each other, mixing with the oppressive heat and sand, always sand. "There had been weeks of fighting, when everyone had remained indoors, and it seemed to me as though the people were taking a deep breath and breathing a sigh of relief that it was over." Gordon opened his eyes, forcing himself into the present so he wasn't overwhelmed.

"My unit consisted of eight other guys, and we were assigned to patrol and provide security for part of the market. We had to be careful, wary, and alert at all times, but mostly we saw smiling faces and people happy to see us as they scurried through the market, most with an undercurrent of desperation, in a rush to buy what they desperately needed," Gordon explained as Mario took his hand.

"Take it one step at a time," Mario told him.

"We'd been on patrol for hours, watching people and looking for anything suspicious. Of course we saw people behaving strangely at times, and we detained them for search and then let them go when we found nothing."

"What happened?" Mario asked.

Gordon stilled, searching his mind for what was real and what he knew his mind had tried to fill in. "I remember hearing the high-pitched sound of an incoming shell. All of us braced for impact as pandemonium broke out around us. People screamed, and then the shell impacted a short distance from us. The ground shook, sand and bits of shredded canvas filling the air along with propelled debris. I remember running with the platoon toward the source of the shelling as another shell came in." Gordon cradled his head in his hands. "That one went off, and all I remember is guys screaming, me going into a fighting stance, shooting while we took incoming fire." The pressure in his head grew worse, and Gordon thought his eyes were going to explode. "I remember someone running away in my peripheral vision and...."

"It's all right, you don't have to tell me more," Mario said.

"The next thing I remember, I was seated in the back of a Humvee covered in blood, but I was uninjured. Bottles and Stacks were next to me on the floor, a mass of blood, and the rest of the platoon looked like they'd been through hell and back. Most of them were unconscious and all of them had some sort of wound. I sat with Stacks and Bottles, holding their hands. Stacks's chest sounded like he was breathing through his own blood. He died within minutes while I held him, begging him to hang on. Then I turned to Bottles, but his chest was still and his eyes blank. I held his hand, too, until we arrived at the aid station and they were taken away. In a matter of minutes, I lost both of them. They were closer than brothers, they were my family." Gordon's lips started to quiver, but he'd go to hell and back before he'd cry. "The worst thing was that I didn't remember what happened or know how we got to the Humvee. The other guys were out of it, so they couldn't tell me much. The medics were able to tell me how they got us out, but not much else. All I know is that the two people I was closest to in the world are dead and I walked out with barely a scratch."

"Is that when the nightmares began?" Mario asked, and Gordon nodded.

"Of all kinds. There were investigations, with people expecting me to have the answers, but I knew next to nothing. Once that was over, I'd had more than I could take. My nerves were shot and I didn't give a rat's ass anymore. For weeks, all I wanted to do when I saw a gun was beg for my life. I suppressed it, but when my time was up, I was gone. Got my discharge papers and did my best to disappear."

"How long ago was that?"

"A little over a year. I stopped by and saw Stacks's wife and kid. They were as beautiful as he said they were. I saw Bottles's family too, but that was the last contact I really had with anyone other than a few phone calls from a phone no one could trace. I withdrew more and more and then got desperate. That's when I sort of found this place." Gordon knew what Mario had done for him when he'd seen he was living out of his car. "Now I think the Marines are after me because they found out something I don't know about that day, and frankly I don't want to remember. Because if I failed them and got them killed, I don't know if I could live with myself."

"So why did Wally say the people in town looked Navy?" Mario asked.

"Technically the Marines are under the Secretary of the Navy, so a lot of the support functions are performed by the Navy. If I was being hunted for some administrative reason, it would be the Navy doing the hunting." Gordon sat back, feeling very drained. "I don't know if they're here looking for me or not. If they show up, I'll cooperate, but I won't go looking for them."

"Don't you want to know what happened? I would. Good or bad, I think I'd want to know what happened to my friends," Mario said.

Gordon stared daggers at Mario, his temper rising. "I do know what happened to them. They're dead."

Mario put up his hands in surrender. "I didn't mean to upset you." Gordon nodded slowly as Mario lightly stroked his arm. "Dakota and Wally are both on calls, so we're on our own for the evening," Mario told him, and Gordon was grateful for the change of subject.

Gordon lifted himself off the sofa and strode to the kitchen. He opened their sparse refrigerator, found the makings of a halfway decent dinner, and got to work. His mind churned over what he'd told Mario and the blanks in his story. He'd been honest—he truly did not remember what had happened. All he knew was that his companions were injured or dead. He had been covered in blood, not his own, with nothing more than a scratch on him, and of course, the aftermath. Having something to do helped, and Gordon concentrated on his cooking, chopping the vegetables he could find and setting them to cook. He found steaks that Mario must have pulled out, along with a few potatoes. After peeling and cutting them, he set the potatoes to boil. "Dinner won't be fancy," he said, knowing Mario could hear him in the other room.

After a few minutes, Mario encircled his waist with his arms. "Doesn't matter, I know it will be good." Mario lightly kissed the base of his neck, and Gordon shivered with anticipation. "Do you need help?"

"No. Things just need to cook and then I can put the steaks on," Gordon answered and then yawned. He felt drained both physically and mentally. "After dinner, I'll probably go right to bed." Feeling Mario lean his head against his shoulder, Gordon continued working, enjoying the closeness and not wanting to break it. "Would you start the grill?" Gordon asked Mario, and the warmth from behind him vanished. He made sure everything was nearly done before opening the back door and placing the steaks on the grill just outside.

"I can finish these for you," Mario said, and Gordon nodded, leaving him to tend the grill. He finished the mashed potatoes and vegetables, then took everything to the table as Mario brought in the streaks. They got dishes and glasses before sitting down to eat. "I was wondering—have you talked to a professional about your memory loss?" Mario asked after swallowing his first bite of steak.

"Yeah. I met with doctors and even a hypnotist, but they couldn't help me. The shrink thought whatever happened was buried so deep I may never remember. He said there are times of extreme stress when the brain forgets to record things and he also said that could have happened. He said there's a lot about memory that we don't know." Gordon looked down at his plate and began eating. "I suppose it would be good to remember. At least I'd know what I did."

Mario swallowed. "If you want my opinion, I think whatever happened was traumatic, but I doubt you did anything you should be ashamed of."

"How do you know?" Gordon asked with more intensity than he intended.

"Because I know you." Mario popped a carrot into his mouth. "You don't do things by half and you have integrity."

"Yeah, I have so much integrity I tried to break onto the ranch and let Wally's cats loose," Gordon said sarcastically, still beating himself up over his poor judgment. He should have known it wasn't right to trespass on someone's property, no matter the reason.

"You had been convinced the animals were in danger, and when you found out they weren't, you owned up to what you'd done," Mario said. "Stop beating yourself up over one mistake." Mario returned to his dinner, and Gordon ate quietly. "It doesn't do any good to stew."

Gordon nearly growled, but kept quiet and continued eating. He wasn't in the mood for conversation any longer. Thankfully, Mario became quiet as well, and they finished their dinners in silence. Once they were done, Gordon cleared the table and did the dishes, putting everything away before turning out the kitchen light and heading to bed. He was exhausted and needed some time alone to think. He cleaned up and then got undressed before climbing into his own bed. As he lay staring at the ceiling, he heard Mario moving through the house. Eventually, he heard him come down the hall. Water ran in the bathroom and then a door closed, followed by silence. Rolling over, Gordon closed his eyes, but sleep wouldn't come no matter how badly he wanted it to or how bone tired he was.

Gordon rolled over for what seemed like the millionth time. Pushing back the covers in a huff, he rolled over again, trying to get comfortable, but nothing was working. He got out of bed and opened the door before looking into the hallway. Then he left his room and quietly stepped to Mario's. Mario had left the door cracked, and when Gordon peered inside, he saw Mario staring back at him. Gordon pushed open the door, and Mario lifted the covers, immediately holding him close when he climbed in beside him. Gordon closed his eyes and almost instantly fell asleep.

GORDON sat behind a table, facing a group of three officers in dress uniforms. They all stared at him sternly but didn't say a word. "You know what you did," an unseen voice said accusingly. "You weren't watching where you were shooting." Gordon looked around to see where the voice had come from, but saw only blackness around him.

"I don't remember anything," Gordon said, but deep down he accepted what they said as true. "I truly don't remember any of it at all, sirs." He spoke to the tribunal, who continued their stony silence.

"You could remember everything if you wanted to, but you don't. Your forgetfulness only proves your guilt. You don't want to remember because you know you're guilty," the unseen voice went on, and this time the members of the tribunal, whose faces he couldn't really see no matter how hard he tried, nodded their heads slowly.

"Do you know what happened?" Gordon asked the tribunal, and they stopped moving. "Do you?" he yelled to the unseen voice, but all remained silent. "I have no memory of what happened!" Gordon yelled. "I can't remember! I wish I could, but I can't." He felt trapped behind his table and tried to stand up, but couldn't move no matter how hard he tried.

"You must," the voice said, this time much more slowly. "Your friends can never rest until you do," the voice said, and Gordon gasped as the tribunal nodded slowly once again. This time he could see them clearly and they had no faces, only forms that slowly faded to nothing. Gordon gasped, his eyes flying open to be met by darkness. At first he thought he was still there.

"It's okay, Gordon, it was only a dream," Mario soothed, and Gordon felt him lightly stroke his arm. "You're okay." Mario gently tugged him back onto the mattress. "Was it the kind of dream you usually have?"

"No." Gordon thought, trying to remember if anything like that had actually happened. "I was in a sort of court, but I couldn't move. They accused me of shooting my friends, and I couldn't remember anything. They said I could remember if I wanted to, and that my not being able to remember was proof of my guilt."

Mario continued stroking his arm. "Dreams are our minds working through things, nothing more. You're afraid you might have done something you can't remember, so your mind is visualizing that fear. It's nothing to worry about. It's got no basis in reality, only your fear." Mario continued stroking him. Gordon turned over to face Mario, and he kissed him lightly. "Close your eyes and try to go back to sleep. It was just a dream."

Gordon nodded slowly and closed his eyes once again. It was only a dream, but what if it was his mind's way of telling him that his worst fears were correct, that he had done something to harm his friends? Gordon couldn't seem to let it go and remained awake for much of the night.

Chapter Six

THE ranch had been quiet, almost unusually quiet, for the past week. The lighting was wired, set, and working beautifully. If anyone tried to get at the cats, they'd be bathed in light that could be seen from almost anywhere on the ranch. Gordon had somehow wired the lights so that if one was triggered, they all came on. The nightmares Gordon had been having had tapered off, and for the past few nights he'd slept peacefully all night long. And, to Gordon's relief, no one from the military had shown up at the ranch looking for him. Whatever they had been in town to do, it most likely hadn't concerned Gordon, because all they'd needed to do was speak with the sheriff and they'd have known exactly where Gordon was. No, everything was quiet, and that was exactly how Mario liked it. Getting out of his lonely bed, Mario dressed and shaved before wandering outside to where he knew he'd find Gordon—watching the colt frolicking in his paddock with his mother.

"You could have stayed in bed a little longer," Mario said as he approached, but Gordon just shrugged.

"I learned to get up early and can't seem to stop," Gordon said without looking away from the colt. "Do you know what Dakota and Wally have planned for him?"

Mario chuckled. "Doesn't matter. My job comes with a place for two horses. She happens to be one of mine and so is the colt." As if he knew Mario was talking about him, the colt wandered over, sniffing and looking for treats. Gordon stroked the horse's nose, and the colt snorted before nuzzling his head to Gordon's chest. The colt was certainly taken with Gordon.

"What's the plan for today?" Gordon asked once the colt had moved back toward his mother.

"Finish up your chores in the barn, and then Haven needs help mending some fencing on the east ranges near his house. Some of the posts have weakened and need to be replaced. I also thought that once you were done, we could take a ride to check out some of the cattle in the north range. We can use the ATVs if you like, or take a couple of the horses to see what's going on," Mario said. Gordon had proven himself a reasonably capable rider, but they hadn't had much cause to spend a lot of time riding lately, and Mario was itching to spend some quiet time on the ranges.

"Going by horse would be fine," Gordon said before pushing away from the paddock fence. "I'll get started, then. See you at breakfast." Gordon strode away, and soon Mario heard the sound of a shovel on concrete coming from the barn. He then made his rounds, checking on all the horses and making sure everything was in order. Then he called Haven and arranged for him to pick up Gordon so they could take care of the fences. The other men arrived, and Mario gave them their work for the day according to the plans he and Haven had worked out a few days earlier. He also placed the feed order and ordered other supplies they needed. By the time he was done, Wally hollered that breakfast was ready. So after telling Gordon, he headed inside.

Breakfast was basic and fast. Gordon had finished up his barn work, so he jumped in Haven's truck as soon as he arrived, and they were off. Mario had some repairs he wanted to make to the barn, so he got his tools and supplies before getting down to work.

MARIO worked all morning replacing one of the stall's walls. The late-morning sun heated the barn, so Mario worked bare-chested.

"Well, isn't that a sight," a familiar voice said from behind him. Mario stiffened and slowly stood up, turning around to find David leaning against the doorjamb.

"What are you doing here?" Mario asked as his heart leaped for a few seconds before wariness kicked in. "I thought you were in Montana."

The smile from David's face faltered. "I was up until a few days ago," David said. "Things there turned real sour very fast." David stepped closer. "Everything seemed to fall apart all at once." He stepped closer, stroking Mario's cheek. "I missed you."

Mario closed his eyes, reacting to the familiar touch. "I missed you for a very long time as well," Mario said, carefully taking David's hand in his and moving it away from his face. "I have work to do," Mario said, his head spinning.

"I was hoping you could forgive me," David whispered. "I know I didn't treat you right, but I was hoping you'd give me the chance to make it up to you." Mario stood still, shocked and stunned. "I was a fool to ever leave."

David was standing in front of him asking for forgiveness, something Mario had dreamed of for months. But there was none of the excitement he expected. "We can't just go back to the way things were." Mario grabbed a rag from where he'd put it on a stack of hay bales. "You left me and have been gone eighteen months. I spent all that time trying to get over you, missing you, wishing you'd come back. I finally am able to move on, and here you are telling me you made a mistake." Mario twisted the rag nervously as he wiped his hands. "Well, you did make a mistake, because you left in the first place and threw away the years we had together. I can't pretend you never left."

"I don't expect you to. I'm just asking for you to give me a chance," David pleaded softly.

"I don't know if I can," Mario said honestly.

"There's someone else, isn't there?" David asked jealously.

Mario stepped forward, his temper blazing. "You have no right to ask that, and no fucking right to be jealous. You left me, remember? Yes, there is someone else. We haven't been seeing each other long, but I want to see if there's anything between us. I treated you well, cared for you, loved you no matter what, even after you left." Mario shook his head.

"What's all the yelling?" Wally asked as he stepped into the barn. Mario knew exactly when Wally recognized David because his eyes widened and then hardened to stone.

"Sorry, Wally. David and I were having a discussion. I didn't mean for it to get so loud," Mario said. He saw Wally nod, but his expression didn't soften a bit.

"So what brings you back?" Wally asked, his lips forming a straight line.

"Things didn't work out, and I was hoping you might need some help," David said, slipping his hat off his head.

Wally shook his head. "The ranch has a full complement of hands right now. You might want to check with Steve to see if he and Wilson need anyone. You could also check with Milford. He may need a hand. We'll give you a good reference, but I don't think we can use you here." Wally kept his voice level.

"I guess it was too much to hope for," David said, and Wally nodded.

"Probably was. Check out those places, and if they don't have anything, let us know. We can ask around," Wally said and then strode forcefully out of the barn.

"I guess I should be going," David said, and he too turned to leave.

"Do you have a place to stay?" Mario asked.

"Not really. I sort of foolishly hoped I could stay with you, but...." His gaze followed where Wally had gone. "I think he made it pretty clear that isn't an option." David turned back to Mario.

"Not that I blame him. One of the things I always liked about Wally was his fierce loyalty." David shuffled toward the barn door. "I'll see you around."

Mario watched David leave and then sat on the stacked hay bales, holding his head in his hand. What in hell was he going to do? David was suddenly back, and stuff with Gordon felt so up in the air. He really liked him, but David had been in his life for years. The more he thought about it, the more his head hurt.

"He's gone?" Wally asked, and Mario lifted his head, nodding slowly. "Good." Mario opened his mouth to protest, but Wally sat down next to him. "You and David were together for a number of years, but it was over between the two of you before he left. It's taken you a while to realize that, but I think you know it now. You also know that things will never be the same even if you did take David back. You couldn't trust that he wouldn't find something or someone he thought was better and leave you again." Mario nodded. "David's hurting because what he chased ultimately ended up as an illusion, so he came back with his tail between his legs, and you're the consolation prize."

"You think so?" Mario asked.

"Yes. He didn't love you enough to stay, but he cares enough now to come back when what he chased is gone. No, you're better off without him. Even if Gordon wasn't in the picture, you're better off alone, respect intact, than with David, waiting for him to leave again." Wally grew quiet, and Mario figured he was waiting for him to say something, but he had nothing. He knew everything Wally had said was the truth, but it still didn't lessen his confusion. "I know you and Gordon haven't had much time together, but at this point in your life, which man, David or Gordon, do you know in your heart would walk through fire if you needed him?" Wally stood up and half smiled at him before quietly leaving the barn.

Mario knew Wally was right, but he hated the mixed-up, churning feeling in his stomach. He stood up and went back to work to try to take his mind off it.

IT DIDN'T work very well. Hours later, he'd gotten little done and realized he'd spent most of his energy worrying about what he was going to do. Thankfully, he finished replacing the stall wall hours after he should have and began putting away the tools and supplies. It was quiet around the ranch yard, so Mario went inside and to his bedroom. Pulling open the bottom drawer of his dresser, he hauled out all the pictures of David he'd taken down weeks before. He and David smiled back at him from where they stood in front of Mario's mare, the very one nursing her colt in the paddock. They were happy, the smiles on their faces full and warm. He sighed softly and set the framed photograph aside. Lifting the next one, he stared at a picture of David on horseback. They'd had a good life together and they were happy….

"What's going on?" Gordon asked from the doorway, a slight scowl on his face.

"Just remembering," Mario answered as he gathered the pictures and quickly placed them back in the drawer. He turned toward where Gordon had stood but found the doorway empty. A few seconds later, he flinched as the back door banged closed. He shoved the drawer closed and went outside. He found Gordon standing at the paddock, right where Mario knew he'd be, watching the colt and his mother.

"Do you do that a lot?" Gordon asked without turning to look at Mario.

"What?"

"Look at his picture and pine for him?" Gordon answered, again without looking away from the colt.

"No. I haven't had them out since I took them down," Mario said.

Gordon finally turned to face him. "Then why now?"

Mario swallowed. "David showed up today. He wanted to come back. Wally told him there wasn't a job here for him."

"Did he want you back?" Gordon asked. "Because I won't stand in your way," he added, but Mario saw him grip the fence rail hard enough to turn his knuckles white.

"How noble of you," Mario retorted.

"Well, what do you want me to say?" Gordon asked forcefully.

"The truth," Mario said, staring Gordon in the eye.

"Okay," Gordon said, staring back. "The truth is that if I see David I'll want to tear him to pieces for what he did to you, and it makes me sick to think of you pining away for a man who loved you so much that he left. Yeah, you were happy, I could see that from the pictures on the walls, but things couldn't have been so happy toward the end. I want to rip him to shreds for hurting you." Gordon stepped closer, looming over him. "And I want to smack you upside the head for letting yourself hope and pray for damned near two years that David would come back to you. He fucking left, and now that he's back you're pining for him again." Gordon paused to breathe, and Mario opened his mouth to interrupt, but Gordon cut him off. "You deserve better than being some loser's fallback guy, and he should know better than to come back here wrangling to get back in your bed so he can leave you again when something better comes along."

"David isn't like that," Mario protested without heat.

"He isn't, huh?" Gordon growled. "He did it once and he'll do it again. Leopards don't change their spots."

"Well, according to Wally, their spots do move over time," Mario quipped, and Gordon stared at him, openmouthed. Then Mario smiled to defuse the situation, and Gordon growled deep and low in his throat. "Sorry. I know you're right, and I thought I was over him. I haven't thought of David much in the past few weeks, but then he showed up today and now everything's all twisted up."

"You need to decide what you want and you need to decide pretty darned quick. 'Cause if good old David is going to be spending a lot of time sniffing around you, he's going to have a broken nose and rearranged lips, and the pretty face from those pictures isn't going to be quite so pretty anymore," Gordon said as he pounded the rail with his fist.

"You're a caveman," Mario accused, and Gordon grinned.

"I watch out for my own," Gordon said in a deep, low tone before turning away and striding toward the ranch house. Mario watched him walk around the side of the house. He wasn't sure if he should follow or not, but his legs seemed to have their own ideas.

He found Gordon sitting on the ground near the enclosure they'd recently built, watching a resting lion. "So I'm yours, huh?" Mario said, as if their conversation hadn't been interrupted.

"Yup," Gordon said without looking at him. Mario thought for a few seconds and found he liked that idea. "Whether you know it or not." Gordon turned away from the lion, looking deep into his eyes. "This David guy doesn't have a hold on your heart any longer, because you let him go. But if you really want him back, then you better say so now. You asked for the truth earlier and I gave it to you." Gordon lunged toward him, and Mario fell backward onto the grass. "If you want me to stop, you better say so now," Gordon told him.

All Mario could manage was to shake his head before Gordon's lips were on his and he started opening Mario's belt. Within seconds, Gordon was devouring his mouth and had his pants open, underwear down, gripping his cock like he was never going to let him go. Mario groaned and closed his eyes while Gordon took possession of his mouth.

The rough grass scratched his skin where his shirt had ridden up, but he really didn't give a damn. Mario thrust his hips and Gordon gripped him tighter, stroking hard and firm. "That's it," he said.

"More," Mario moaned wantonly.

Gordon stroked him furiously fast as Mario went from zero to a hundred within seconds. His focus contracted to only what Gordon was doing to him and the depth of Gordon's eyes. "Come for me, Mario, right here, right now!"

Mario bit his lower lip as the primal portions of his brain took over. Within seconds, Mario gasped for breath, his body going into overdrive, and he came hard, shooting over Gordon's hand and onto his stomach and shirt. His eyes remained closed as he collapsed back onto the tall grass, gasping for breath through his open mouth. Gordon loosened his grip and then slipped away. Slowly, Mario opened his eyes to find Gordon staring intently back. "The next time you think about David, remember that." Gordon nodded once for emphasis and then moved away, watching as Mario put himself back together and did his best to wipe the come stains off his shirt.

"Leave it," Gordon said. "That's physical proof of how I make you feel and what I do to you." Gordon stood up and waited until Mario was reasonably presentable before offering his hand and tugging him to his feet. Then Gordon pulled Mario against his body. "I bet David never made you feel that way," Gordon said before pulling him into a bruising kiss. Then he backed away, striding across the range and around the side of the ranch house. Over the past weeks, Mario had noticed that Gordon's confidence seemed to be building, and over that time, he saw more and more of the Marine in him. The one thing he hadn't counted on was how much it turned him on. Gordon had just wrung a mind-blowing orgasm out of him, but watching Gordon stride across the land full of confidence already had him half-hard again.

Mario checked himself over and then followed, his legs a bit unsteady. As he rounded the side of the house, he saw David's truck parked in the drive. Gordon was nowhere in sight. He thought about trying to find both men, but decided it would probably be best to change his shirt before he advertised to everyone what he and Gordon had been up to.

He pulled open the door to the foreman's house and stepped into the middle of a war. Gordon stood on one side of the kitchen table, arms folded across his chest, staring daggers at David, who stood on the other side, a bundle of flowers on the table in front of him.

"Who is this?" David asked without turning his head.

"What are you doing in here?" Mario asked, ignoring David's question. "You don't live here any longer, remember?"

"I haven't had any luck finding a job and I came in to wait for you to ask if I could use the sofa for a few days," David said. To his credit, Gordon kept quiet, but Mario figured he was two seconds from flying over the table.

"Okay. First thing, this is Gordon and he lives here too. I somehow doubt he's going to allow you to stay. And secondly, you could have asked before barging into my home—our home," he corrected. The two men continued staring at each other, and Mario would have thought it was funny if he hadn't been afraid Gordon was going to rip David's arms off. "That's enough!" he said to the two of them. "David, I suggest you go."

For a second, Mario thought David was going to protest, but then he turned and slowly left the house. As soon as the door closed, Gordon scooped up the flowers and dumped them into the trash. Then, without a word, he strode into the kitchen, and Mario jumped slightly when Gordon banged one of the pots onto the stove. "You don't have to bring the house down," Mario said lightly.

Gordon whirled toward him. "I walked in here, and he must have thought I was you because he stood just inside the door with those damned flowers."

"It's all right," Mario soothed, his wishes becoming clearer by the minute.

"No, it's not. He doesn't live here anymore and he doesn't own you." Gordon filled the pot with water and banged it back on the stove, spilling onto the burner.

"Yes, it is all right. There's no need to get yourself upset. I somehow doubt David is going to be hanging around here much from now on." Mario stopped and let that thought sink in, wondering how he felt about that. To his surprised relief, he didn't really care. "David's in the past. Some happy, some sad and hurtful, but he's the past." He believed that. All this time he'd hoped, pined, and prayed for David to come back, but now he realized that wasn't what he wanted, or at least he didn't think that was what he wanted.

"Are you sure?" Gordon asked tentatively.

"The honest answer is that I truly believe so," Mario answered. "I figured when I saw David again, I'd feel about him the way I did when we were together and things were good. I don't. In fact, I don't feel much at all. It's like I've been looking and waiting for a ghost all this time."

"Okay," Gordon said and returned his attention to making dinner.

"Do you need help?" Mario asked.

"I'm fine," Gordon said, and Mario figured he needed something to do, so he left him alone and went to his bedroom. He pulled off his shirt and threw it into the laundry basket. Then he grabbed a clean one from the closet and shrugged into it. As he buttoned the shirt, his fingers slowed and then stopped. Gordon cared about him. The thought hit him all of a sudden. He might have a rather basic way of showing it, but he did care for him. Mario smiled slightly at the thought, and within seconds, the smile had turned to a grin.

Mario tucked in his shirt and left the room, following the scent of dinner through the house. His stomach rumbled as he got closer to the kitchen. Gordon was cooking up a storm with multiple pots on the stove and something else in the oven. "I figured I'd cook up some things for the next few days that we can just heat up," Gordon said as he checked one of the pots.

Gordon tended to cook when he was upset or needed to think. Mario had figured that out a while ago and he let him work through the encounter with David. "What are we having?"

"Pasta with meat sauce, and I have garlic bread in the oven," Gordon explained as he took one of the pots off the stove and drained it into the sink. Mario set the table, and then rather than hover, he turned on the television and relaxed while Gordon finished cooking and brought the food to the table.

A knock on the door made Mario smile. "That must be Wally. Dakota's at the hospital today, so I bet he's wondering what's for dinner," Mario said as he got up and walked to the door. When he opened it, he indeed saw Wally, with two men in crisp blue uniforms standing behind him.

"These gentlemen came to the house looking for Gordon," Wally said before entering. Mario glanced into the kitchen. Gordon nodded, and Mario stepped back so all three of them could come inside.

"We're about to sit down for dinner," Mario explained.

"You're Gordon Fisher?" one of the uniformed men asked as he turned to Gordon, who wiped his hands and stepped out of the kitchen after turning everything off.

"Yes," Gordon answered.

"I'm Commander Ross and this is Commander Greer. We need you to come with us," Commander Ross said. Gordon glanced at Mario and Wally before stepping forward.

"What's this about?" Mario asked.

"We aren't at liberty to say," Commander Ross said in a monotone.

"Is he under arrest?" Mario pressed.

"No," Commander Ross answered.

"Then he isn't going anywhere. You can arrange a time for him to come into town to speak with you, but that's all. He isn't in the military any longer. He's a private citizen, and therefore you can't order him to do anything." Mario turned to Wally. "I know you and Dakota have a lawyer—would you give him a call?"

Wally pulled out his phone and scrolled through the numbers.

"We've had a difficult time locating Mr. Fisher, and…."

"That's not his problem. That's yours. As I said, you can make arrangements to talk to him like civilized people or leave." Mario pointed toward the door.

They two men whispered between themselves. "We're working out of the sheriff's office in town. Can you be there at eight in the morning?"

"Of course," Gordon answered. The two men talked softly again.

"Then we'll see you then," Commander Ross said, and they both headed for the door. Wally followed them out.

"Why did you do that?" Gordon asked once the door had closed behind them.

"You're not the only one who takes care of his own," Mario answered. "You are a private citizen, and they have no right to order you to go anywhere. The sheriff could take you in for questioning, but he wasn't here. They can ask what they want to ask tomorrow, and you can have a lawyer present if you want."

Wally came back inside as Mario expected he would, and set another place at the table. "I wasn't able to get in touch with the lawyer, but I left a message. He'll call me back." Wally turned to Gordon. "What do you want me to tell him?"

"I don't know," Gordon said as he brought the last of the food to the table. "Explain what happened and that I may need him."

They all sat down at the table and began to eat. Mario noticed that Gordon picked at his food, eating very little. "You'll find out what they want in the morning," Mario said, and Gordon nodded, eating a bit more.

"David stopped by the house a while ago," Wally said, changing the subject. "He didn't have a place to go. Haven and Phillip are going to put him up for a few days." Wally took a bite of garlic bread. "I think he's getting a little desperate. The guy he was with ran off with most of his money, and then his job dried up just when he needed it most." Wally alternated looking at both of them. "David worked here for a number of years and, yes, he left, but I don't want to see him without a place to stay."

From the expression on his face, Gordon didn't really care, but he nodded his agreement, probably to be nice. Mario felt for David but was glad he wasn't staying here—it would have made things way too complicated. "I know. It's just hard having him back here," Mario said before returning to his dinner.

"I know, but we help our friends, even the one who happen to be assholes sometimes. Haven and Phillip have agreed to put him to work at their place for a few days, so he won't be around here." Wally took a small bite of the garlic bread. "And you know Haven. He'll keep him busy as hell."

The rest of the meal passed in relative, blessed silence. Mario wasn't sure how many more surprises he could take. Once they were done, Mario cleared the table and did the dishes with Wally's help. They sent Gordon in to the living room to relax. When the cleanup was done, Wally said good night, leaving them alone.

Gordon had been watching television, but he switched it off. "I'll need to be up early if I'm going to get some of the chores done before I go to town."

"Hey, you don't have to face this alone," Mario said.

Gordon stared at him for a few seconds. "Yes, I do," he said and left the room.

Mario watched him go, figuring he'd give him a few minutes alone. He finished the cleanup and turned out the lights. Then he too headed to bed. When he found his room empty, Mario was a bit surprised, but he probably shouldn't have been. He and Gordon had slept in the same bed every night for over a week and the empty spot on Gordon's side looked wrong. He marched across the hall and pushed open the door to Gordon's room. "No, you don't," Mario said into the dark room.

"Don't what?" Gordon asked, and Mario sat on the edge of the bed.

"You don't have to do this alone," Mario clarified.

"Actually, I do."

"No, you don't!" Mario said emphatically. "When you go into town, I'll go with you, and while they ask you what they want to ask, I'll be waiting out front. I may not be able to go in with you, but I will be there for you." Mario leaned closer to the reclined form under the sheet. "You aren't alone anymore."

Gordon reached for him, pulling him onto the bed, and their lips met in what felt like desperation. Within seconds, Mario found himself on his back, Gordon pressing him into the mattress while Gordon almost frantically pulled off his clothes. Where his clothes ended up, Mario didn't know or care, because soon they were skin to skin.

Slow tenderness was almost completely absent from Gordon's touch. Instead, there was need, worry, and desperation, like this could be their last time together. Mario had little doubt that he'd have bruises in the morning, but he could tell this was what Gordon needed. He was almost silent as their bodies joined in a whoosh of nearly unbridled passion and a chronic need on both their parts that lasted until sweet release claimed them.

"Sorry," Gordon whispered as he lay on his back next to Mario, their hands entwined. "I didn't mean to hurt you."

Mario released Gordon's hand and rolled onto his side, placing his palm over Gordon's heart. "You didn't. I'm not fragile, and you won't break me. Part of caring for another person is giving them what they need. And you know you're with the right person when you're willing and able to give them what they need when they need it." Mario waited for Gordon's response, but heard nothing. He didn't really need words. Gordon was pretty good at making his feelings known without words.

Mario closed his eyes but sleep wouldn't come. His mind churned over the events of the day. When David had shown up, his thoughts and emotions had been muddled, but what he hadn't anticipated was that David's appearance would help clarify his feelings for Gordon. They were clearer to him than they'd ever been, but that also scared him half to death. The last time he'd felt this way, it hadn't ended well. He knew all he could do was hope this time it didn't end up the way it had with David. With that settled, he cleared his mind somewhat before shifting to worry about what the Navy wanted with Gordon.

Chapter Seven

GORDON was in the courtroom again, the same faceless, silent panel stared at him, but this time his accuser was in the room with him—Commander Ross. "You can remember if you want to," he kept saying, and Gordon did his best to maintain control. But Commander Ross's hounding became too much.

"I can't remember!" Gordon shouted, pounding the table with his fist until it broke in half and fell to pieces.

Still, Commander Ross continued. "You can remember if you want to," he kept saying, and no matter how hard Gordon denied it, he wouldn't stop. "You can remember, you can remember." Soon the members of the tribunal were chanting it as well, the first words they had uttered. Gordon then realized they were getting closer, everyone in the room was getting closer, until they surrounded him, standing over him, continually chanting, "You can remember, but you don't want to."

The chanting stopped and Gordon gasped for breath, holding his head. "You can remember, but you don't want to because you're guilty," Ross said as clear as a bell, and Gordon lunged for him, catching him around the throat.

"Gordon, it's me!" Someone shook him hard, and he opened his eyes. Gordon found himself on top of Mario. "It's all right, it's just me. You were dreaming!" Mario gripped his wrists, and Gordon realized he'd been choking Mario. "You're all right," Mario told him, and Gordon released his hands and jumped off the bed, shaking like a leaf.

"I could have killed you," Gordon said, still trying to catch his breath.

"No, you wouldn't," he said, but the veracity of his words was called into question when Mario rubbed his throat. "What happened?"

The dream images were already fading from his memory. "It was the court dream again, but this time they cornered me. One of the special agents was there, and he wouldn't let up." Gordon backed away, leaning against the wall, afraid to get too close to Mario and half expecting him to leave the room at any moment. "He came at me, and I lunged for him in my dream."

Mario nodded slowly. "It's all right. I know you didn't mean to hurt me."

"But I could have," Gordon said.

"These commanders, the PTSD, combined with the memory loss, are all churning around in your head. During the day, you have something to keep your mind occupied, but when you sleep it all comes out. It's to be expected."

"I want it to get better," Gordon said futilely.

"It may never go away. But I suspect that once your mind conjures up what you can't remember you'll feel a lot better, and the dreams will dissipate because the doubt won't hold sway any longer." Mario climbed back under the covers and motioned toward him. Gordon hesitated. "Come back to bed. We're both fine, and you need some rest."

Gordon went to the bed, lying down again, but he stayed away from Mario as best he could, until Mario rolled over and curled against his side. Reluctantly, Gordon closed his eyes, not trusting himself. But eventually he fell back to sleep.

GORDON woke later than he'd intended, so he rushed to get his most urgent chores completed before grabbing a quick bite to eat. Mario was waiting for him and drove him into town. They parked in the visitor parking of the sheriff's office. Out in front, Gordon stood staring at the nondescript building, telling himself he was a Marine and to act like it. After lifting his shoulders and straightening his back, he marched up the stairs and pulled open the door. A woman in uniform sat behind a bulletproof window, and Gordon gave her his name. "It'll be just a minute," she said with a smile before disappearing behind a partition. Gordon turned and sat down next to Mario.

"You look like a Marine," Mario told him quietly. "I like it. The confidence looks good on you." The woman opened the door and motioned for Gordon to come forward. "I'll be here waiting for you," Mario told him.

"Thanks," Gordon said and walked through the door to the room the woman indicated. Inside, Commanders Ross and Greer were waiting for him. They both stood, and Gordon waited. "What can I help you with?" Gordon asked as he took the chair that was obviously meant for him. They both sat down.

"You are Gordon Aaron Fisher, formerly of the Marine Corps?" Commander Ross asked.

"Yes. I told you that last night," Gordon answered. "Can we dispense with the military bullshit and get down to why you asked me to come here? I have work to do."

"What we'd like you to do is tell us what happened on the afternoon of April 24, 2011, in the market in Fallujah," Commander Ross asked.

"I assume you have the reports from the initial investigation," Gordon said. "I have no more to add than what's in there."

Commander Ross opened a file folder and set it on the table. "There are many questions you were unable to answer. Critical questions that the Marines would like answers to."

"I can't give them answers because I do not remember. Those portions of what happened are a complete blank. I remember the shells hitting the market and I remember the shooting. The next thing I know, my best friends in the world are dead, the rest of my unit is wounded, and I'm covered in blood that isn't my own, riding in the back of a Humvee to the aid station. I've thought of that day for months and I do not remember anything more. It's like my brain stopped recording what was happening." Gordon looked to both men and saw skepticism on their faces.

"Could it be that you're hiding something?" Commander Ross asked as he leaned over the table, getting in Gordon's space. It was an old trick used often in basic training. It didn't affect him at all.

"I can't hide what I don't know," Gordon answered simply before staring straight ahead. "Like I've said repeatedly, I don't recall anything that happened between the shelling and riding in the Humvee. I've tried for months to make sense of it, but I can't." Gordon paused. "Why is all this coming up again? I was under the impression that the investigation into the incident was closed."

"It's been reopened," Commander Ross said firmly, "at the request of the Secretary of the Navy."

That wasn't good. Gordon had no idea what more he could tell these men. He wanted to help, he really did, because if he could piece together what happened, then maybe he could put his mind to rest. "I wish I could help, but I can't."

"You can remember if you want to," the commander pressed, almost exactly like his dream, and Gordon swallowed hard, pushing back a repeat of the panic he'd felt the night before.

"And you can go to hell," Gordon said, standing up.

"Sit down!" Commander Ross said sharply.

"Am I under arrest?" Gordon asked. When the commander shook his head, Gordon said, "Then we're done. Give me a card, and if I remember anything, I'll call you, but I don't have the information you seem to think I do. As for sitting here wasting time going over old information, forget it." Gordon waited for Commander Ross to produce a card. Gordon took it and then strode toward the door. "I truly do not know how I can help you." Gordon pulled open the door, then closed it behind him before taking a deep breath and heading back the way he'd come.

He passed the woman at the desk and waited for her to buzz him out. Mario stood when he entered the lobby, and Gordon walked directly to the exit and out into the sunshine. "What did they want?" Mario asked from behind him.

"To talk about what I don't remember," Gordon snapped. "They asked the same questions I've been asked before. The asshole even accused me of forgetting things on purpose." Gordon paced the sidewalk until he heard the door open and saw the two agents come out of the building. Then he strode directly to Mario's truck and got inside. He'd had more than enough of this whole business. The incident they kept hashing over had been one of the worst days of his life. What he did remember was bad enough—Gordon didn't need to remember more and add to the pain of what he already felt. Mario joined him in the truck and started the engine. They pulled out of the lot, driving past the agents. Gordon's gaze followed them, and he noticed they watched him until he couldn't see them any longer.

Blessedly, they didn't speak on the drive back, and when they arrived at the ranch, Gordon got out of the truck and went right to work. At this point, he'd do anything to try to make all this go away. "You know, maybe forgetting and trying to keep the memories at bay aren't the answer," Mario said from behind Gordon while he finished in one of the stalls.

"So you think I should dwell on what I can't remember?" Gordon said sarcastically. "I've done that plenty. It hasn't helped shit."

"No," Mario said, then fumbled for words. "Sorry. I guess I want to help but I don't know how."

Gordon stopped what he was doing and turned to Mario. "You are helping by being there." Not knowing what else to say and definitely not in the mood to get mushy, he went back to work.

"Mario," Wally called into the barn, and then Gordon heard rushed footsteps. "Those damned eco people were at it again. They didn't get to the enclosures this time, but we found cut fences and signs where they tried to bring in ATVs or something. What are we going to do? They don't seem to want to stop and they're going to get themselves or some innocent people hurt, not to mention the animals." Wally was clearly upset, and for his sake, Gordon didn't say anything when David appeared in the barn doorway behind him. Gordon did glance at Mario, who looked decidedly uncomfortable.

"Did you call the sheriff?" Gordon asked, and Wally shook his head. "He needs to know." Wally nodded.

"I'll go take a look at that fence," Mario said, already heading toward the barn door.

"I'll help you if you like," David offered, and Gordon saw Mario look at him as though he were asking permission.

"Go ahead," Gordon said. He wasn't sure he liked the idea of them spending time together, but if Mario still had feelings for David, and Gordon was positive he did, maybe the two of them talking would help clear the air. Yes, he could feel his jealousy and more than a little anger rising at the thought of them alone together, but he tamped it down. His feelings for Mario were becoming clearer and clearer to him, but he was not going to leave Mario's residual feelings for David hanging over his head.

Mario stepped closer. "Are you sure?" he whispered.

"Yes. Go ahead." Gordon turned to Wally, and he seemed to understand, ushering David out of the barn as he went. "Take care of what you need to and talk things over with David. It's best."

Mario nodded and turned to leave the barn. He was nearly at the door when Gordon hurried up to him, turned Mario around, and pressed him against one of the stall walls, kissing him hard and deep. Mario moaned softly, and Gordon deepened the kiss to knee-weakening level. "What was that for?" Mario asked, and Gordon saw him swallow hard after breaking the kiss.

"When you're out there with him, I wanted you to have something to remember," Gordon growled softly.

Mario swallowed again and nodded slowly. Gordon backed away and watched Mario leave the barn. A short time later, he heard two ATVs start up and then listened as the engine sounds softened with distance. Gordon wasn't sure he'd done the right thing, not one bit.

He'd intended to return to work, but wandered out to the paddock instead. Leaning against the fence, he watched the colt and mare as he frolicked and she ate. Eventually, the colt returned to nurse for a while, and Gordon went back inside to get back to work.

"GORDON," Wally called into the barn a while later, and Gordon put aside his tools and followed the voice. The sheriff himself stood next to Wally, a huge man with almost the look of an old-time lawman. Gordon half expected him to have six-shooters at his hips.

"Is there something I can help you with?"

The sheriff looked decidedly uncomfortable. "These eco people are more determined than I thought, and I'm not happy to admit that we haven't been able to get a handle on them. The men you caught were able to tell us little more than you did, and we haven't been able to catch up with the ringleaders. Now Wally says that they've tried again."

"I've given it some thought," Gordon said. "I think they may have been on a reconnaissance mission of some kind. From what

Wally said, they didn't get close enough to trip the lights, but I figure since the last two times they tried, they failed, this time they're spending more time getting the lay of the land. That's what I would do. Hell, if I'm honest, that's what I should have done the first time. Then I wouldn't have done something stupid."

"What we need is someone we can try to get on the inside," the sheriff said thoughtfully. "They always seem to pick drifter types and people who seem down on their luck." The sheriff looked at Gordon expectantly.

"They aren't going to let me anywhere near them again," Gordon said, and the sheriff nodded his agreement even as an idea began to form in Gordon's mind. "Did they pick up the men at the same place they found me?" Gordon asked.

"The greasy-spoon diner just north of town, yeah," the sheriff answered, and Gordon nodded. "You have the look of a man with an idea."

"Maybe," Gordon answered even as the idea continued to churn and take shape.

"Do you want to tell me about it?" the sheriff pressed.

Gordon met the sheriff's eyes. "Not yet," Gordon answered. He didn't know the man or really trust him, so Gordon decided he'd let his idea stew for a bit and then talk it over with Wally, Dakota, and Mario. The sheriff scowled, but Gordon ignored it, shifting his attention to Wally.

"If we think of anything or have any ideas that might help, we'll call you," Wally said. "Could I interest you in a cup of coffee or something cold to drink?" The sheriff declined, but Gordon noticed how Wally had easily defused the situation.

"I best be going," the sheriff said before heading toward his car.

"Appreciate you stopping by," Wally said, and Gordon waited until he was gone before going back to work.

He kept himself busy for the rest of the morning before eating a quick lunch. He spent the afternoon completing everything on his list of chores, looking at his watch every five minutes and wondering where Mario was and what he and David were talking about. Once he'd done all he could, Gordon went inside, but quickly found he was looking out the window at every sound, hoping it was Mario. Finally, he gave up and wandered over to the main house.

Wally answered his knock and ushered him inside. "What's got you all stirred up?" Wally asked after getting them each a beer and settling on the sofa. "And don't tell me you're worried about Mario and David. You did the right thing. Let them talk through the junk between them and maybe make some peace."

"I know it's the right thing. But Mario's spent months wishing David were back and now he is. What if he jumps at the chance?"

Wally stilled, staring at him for a full minute. Gordon had spent time with drill sergeants, men whose job it was to intimidate, but he hadn't felt like squirming until he felt Wally's intense gaze on him. "Have you told him how you feel?" Gordon shrugged before shaking his head. "You know it isn't weak or un-Marine-like to tell someone what you feel about them. Sometimes it's what people need to hear in order to help them work through their own feelings."

Gordon knew Wally was probably right, but he wasn't ready to tell Mario how he felt. Hell, he still wasn't sure himself. When he didn't answer, Wally huffed softly and took a pull from his beer. "Everything is going to be fine," Wally told him.

They sat in silence for a while, drinking their beer. A million things ran through Gordon's mind, none of them good in relation to what was currently happening with Mario and David. Finally, he heard footsteps on the porch. He turned, hoping it was them, but Dakota came inside. He got a beer and joined them, sitting next to Wally, and the two of them instantly curled around each other. "Thanks for the beer, Wally," Gordon said before leaving them alone.

He went out to the paddock and watched the mare and colt. He stood there for quite a while, until he felt arms slide around his waist. "You okay?" Mario asked softly into his ear.

"Yeah, just waiting for you," Gordon answered, lolling his head back slightly to rest on Mario's shoulders. "Did you get the fences fixed?"

"Yeah, but it was a pain. They did a number on the wire and the posts, so we had to replace quite a bit." Mario sighed tiredly.

"Did you two talk?" Gordon asked, figuring he might as well come to what he was worried about.

"Yes. We agreed that what we had between us was in the past. We still care for each other, but things can never be the same way. My feelings have changed, and so have his. But I think we can be friends. Not that I want him working here, or to see him every day, but I think I can let history be history." Mario squeezed him a little tighter. "Is that what's had you all wound up?"

Gordon turned in Mario's embrace. "Am I that open to everyone? Wally asked me the same kind of thing a while ago."

"Only to the people who care about you," Mario answered.

"Where's David now?"

"He headed back to Phillip and Haven's once we were done, and I think he's going to be moving on soon."

"No," Gordon said, and Mario looked confused. "I mean, I had this idea I wanted to run by you, and it involves David." Gordon took a minute to gather his thoughts. "The sheriff came by, and he isn't making any headway catching the people who put me up to trying to release Wally's cats. They seem to appear and then vanish again. I thought if David was willing, he could pose as a hard-luck case at the diner where they found me and they might contact him. He hasn't been around here in a while. None of us can do it, but maybe he could."

"You mean an undercover operation?" Mario teased.

"If you don't think it's a good idea, you can just say so instead of poking fun," Gordon sniped.

"I wasn't, and I don't think it can hurt if David's willing. But the most important kind of undercover operation I want to talk about doesn't involve him." Mario pulled him closer and lightly nibbled his ear. "I was thinking that my bed inside has covers and maybe we should get under them for a while. I'm done for the day, and from what I saw in the barn, you are too." Mario released his ear, then sucked lightly on the skin at the base of his neck. Gordon tried to swallow the moan that threatened but failed. "I like that sound." Gordon tensed slightly. "You know, there's no shame in showing someone how they make you feel. And for that matter, there's nothing weak in allowing yourself to be cared for."

Gordon knew that. It wasn't weakness he was concerned about—it was giving up control. As long as he had that, he wouldn't again feel like he had when he'd come back to himself in the Humvee with his best friends dead. He hadn't been in control of anything then and he'd never been so scared and unsure of himself in his life. He never wanted to feel that way again. "It's not that," Gordon said softly, forcing his body to relax.

"Then let it go. Let everything go and trust me," Mario whispered, licking his skin with just enough force to make him shiver.

Gordon wasn't sure he could do it, but he wanted to. Wherever Mario touched him, his skin came alive, and he wanted to feel that way everywhere. "I'll try."

"You know I'd never hurt you," Mario said, and Gordon nodded. "So let me show you what you mean to me. This isn't you and me fucking around. What we have, what we feel, is more than that. Or at least what *I* feel is more than that."

Gordon swallowed. "It's more than that for me too."

"Then part of feeling that way is trust, both getting and giving. So I'm asking you to trust me. If you don't like something, we can stop, but I can guarantee you'll like what I have in mind. I promise." Mario popped open the top buttons of Gordon's shirt, sliding his hand over Gordon's chest, fingers teasing one of his nipples and sending little zings up his spine. "Let's go inside. We don't want to put on a show." Mario moved away and took Gordon's hand, leading him across the yard and into the house. They barely had the door closed before Mario was tugging him down the hall and into his bedroom.

Mario closed the door and stood in front of him, raking his gaze over Gordon from head to toe. If Mario had been a stranger, Gordon would have growled or puffed himself up to make himself look bigger until they stopped, but with Mario, his entire body thrummed and his pants became nearly impossibly tight. Mario stepped closer, and Gordon reached for him.

"Nope, right now I'm in charge, so you let me take care of you," Mario chastised lightly before, button by button, he opened Gordon's shirt. Mario slid his hands over Gordon's shoulders, pushing his shirt out of the way and off his arms. The fabric hung around his waist, and Gordon started to pull the shirt out of his pants so he could cast it aside, but Mario glided his hands over his chest, stroking his skin with an amazingly light touch that left him wanting more, and Gordon forgot all about his shirt. "You like that, don't you?" Mario asked as he tweaked one of his nipples. "*They* certainly do." He did it again. "They're hard," Mario whispered before leaning forward, sucking on one and then the other.

Gordon arched his back, thrusting his chest into Mario's face, desperate for more. Mario gave him more, sucking and licking him until he could barely stand it.

Gordon's jeans hit the floor. He'd been so engrossed in what Mario was doing with his lips he hadn't paid attention as Mario opened his pants. But he was aware as soon as his pants slid away and Mario lightly rubbed him through the fabric of his boxers. Gordon groaned from deep in his throat, and Mario rubbed harder before pushing the fabric aside, stroking the bare skin of his cock.

"Jesus," Gordon said as his leg began to vibrate.

Mario smiled evilly and gently pushed him backward. Gordon stepped back until he encountered the bed, and Mario continued pressing until Gordon found himself on his back looking up at Mario with a touch of surprise. "Do you have any idea how decadent you look right now?" Mario asked him.

"No," Gordon answered, shifting his attention to himself.

"Well, you do," Mario told him as he slowly climbed onto the bed. "Half in and half out of your clothes, that surprised expression in your eyes, the way your mouth hangs open just a little, even the slightly flushed color to your skin. All of it completely decadent. If I didn't know better, I'd almost say you'd been thoroughly fucked."

Gordon swallowed and closed his eyes. "You know, I don't think...."

"I wasn't asking you to. I simply said you looked it, and believe me, that's a compliment." Mario tugged off his shirt and then straddled Gordon's legs, gripping his cock once again. Without letting go, Mario leaned forward, sucking on a nipple as he continued stroking. "I told you I would make you feel good," Mario said. "Do you trust me?"

Gordon hesitated for a split second. "Yes," he answered softly.

"Good," Mario said, and the evil look returned. Mario released his cock and slid down his body, kissing and licking trails over his chest and stomach. As Mario got closer to his cock, Gordon began thrusting his hips slightly, desperate to have Mario touch him again. Gordon's mouth went dry and he held his breath, waiting in sweet anticipation for Mario's touch. It didn't come, or at least not in the way he expected.

Mario licked up and down his length and then ran his lips along the ridge of his cock. Back and forth, up and down, he continued moving until Gordon's eyes crossed. Just when he thought he couldn't take it any longer, Mario stopped. Then Gordon was engulfed in the wettest heat of his life. Mario sucked him deep and hard, taking him all the way down his throat before releasing his cock once again.

"I'm not going to last," Gordon warned, feeling a bit ashamed at just how quickly Mario had pushed him to the edge.

"Don't want that to happen... yet," Mario told him mischievously before moving away. Gordon stared as Mario climbed off the bed and stripped off the last of his clothes. Naked, rigid cock waving with each movement, Mario went to the nightstand, and Gordon tensed as he watched Mario pull out a condom and some lube. Trust was one thing, and he did trust Mario, but he wasn't ready for what he thought Mario had in mind. "I asked you to trust me and I meant it," Mario told him quietly. "I want you to relax and take your own advice—let yourself feel and don't worry about anything."

Mario opened the bottle of lube, slicking his fingers. Gordon hissed softly when Mario reached behind himself. He knew where those fingers were going and what they were doing. He also knew what it felt like to have his own fingers buried in Mario's passage. Mario's eyes rolled slightly, and Gordon thought about tugging him forward so he could take over Mario's pleasure. "Be patient," Mario said as if reading his mind.

Both of Mario's hands now visible, Gordon waited to see what Mario had in mind. He didn't have to wait long. Mario climbed back onto the bed, straddling him before rolling his hips. Mario's balls slid up and down his shaft, providing teasing friction that had him bucking almost wildly for more. Mario chuckled and reached over to the nightstand, grabbing the condom. The sound of a quick tear met Gordon's ears, the air bristling with anticipatory energy. Mario stilled, and Gordon gasped as he felt his lover roll the condom down his shaft. "What are you doing?" he asked as his brain seemed to shut down.

"Today I'm driving," Mario told him, reaching for the lube. Mario squeezed more onto his fingers and then gripped Gordon's shaft, hard and firm, stroking up and down, stealing Gordon's breath away. Mario lifted upward, positioning himself, and then slowly Gordon felt himself slide into Mario's body. "Just stay still," Mario said as he placed his hand on Gordon's chest when he tried to thrust forward. Gordon complied and slowly—way too slowly for Gordon's liking—Mario slid down his shaft. Not having the control was bothering him. He almost desperately needed it, but what Mario was doing to him quickly pushed that to the back burner.

Mario's butt settled on his hips, and Gordon stilled, Mario's body pulsing around him while he jumped and throbbed inside Mario's searingly hot body. Gordon growled softly when Mario didn't move. "Move!" Gordon snapped, but all Mario did was smile slightly and tighten the muscles around Gordon, making him growl again.

"Like I said, I'm in the driver seat. Give yourself over to the sensation," Mario told him, slowly lifting his body and then settling back down. It was some movement, but not nearly what Gordon wanted. "Allowing someone else to see to your pleasure is hard. You want what you want, but you get what I give you."

"Pushy bottom," Gordon gasped and thrust forward anyway. But all he did was lift himself and Mario off the bed.

"You're damned right, and you're a controlling top," Mario countered, and damned if he didn't make Gordon wait before moving again. Gordon sighed as Mario rolled his hips back and forth, up and down.

"Feels like you're riding a horse," Gordon gasped.

"I am," Mario answered, moving his hips faster and with more force. Gordon could hardly believe how the same movements felt so much more alive and edgy when he wasn't in control. He'd known his own partners really responded to it. He'd found that out years ago, but to be on the receiving end was new for him. Mario continued moving, and Gordon stroked his hand up and down Mario's chest and then up and down his thighs.

Mario stroked himself, leaning back slightly as he seemed to lose himself in the sensation. Gordon tried to take control, but Mario wouldn't let him, going back to rolling his hips and driving Gordon wild. Gordon knew he wouldn't last much longer if Mario kept this up, and he showed no sign of slowing down.

Gordon felt his release building and then stopped, hanging on the edge. Gordon gripped the sheets as Mario slowed his movements just enough to keep him there for what seemed like forever. Again and again, Gordon thought Mario was going to move faster or harder, give him that little extra bit he needed, and time and time again, Mario kept him right there, balancing on the knife's edge. Then Gordon felt Mario's muscles tighten around him, the speed of his movements picking up, and Mario stroked himself faster and faster, his hand becoming a blur. "I'm almost there," Mario told him, and Gordon hung on as he finally felt himself start to tip over the edge. He was used to controlling his partners, not being controlled.

Mario's threw his head back, and his hot release painting Gordon's chest. That last bit of passion threw him over the edge, and his own release hit him like a tidal wave, crashing hard into his chest. Gordon gasped and then held his breath as he rode the endorphinal waves.

He could barely move or breathe for the longest time, so he lay there, Mario's weight on his legs, their breathing synchronizing as they both recovered from what had threatened to turn Gordon's brains to mush. Slowly he came out of his reverie and opened his eyes. Mario looked as blissful as he felt, still sitting on his body. Without thinking, he tugged Mario forward, kissing him hard as their bodies separated in another burst of sensation. "Thank you," Gordon said, feeling amazing. "You're wonderful."

"Trust is a beautiful thing, isn't it?" Mario asked as he settled on the bed next to him.

Gordon thought for a few seconds and he had to agree. "Yes, it is," he said, and Mario held him closer. Soon, Gordon closed his eyes and that was all he remembered.

Chapter Eight

MARIO woke to an unusual situation. Gordon was still in bed with him and he was being held. The being held part wasn't so unusual, but having Gordon still in bed was. After their lively lovemaking session and a short nap—that was how Mario thought of it, and he hoped Gordon did as well—they'd had dinner and finished some evening chores before returning to the bed for the rest of the evening. Mario smiled as he watched Gordon sleep. Somehow he'd managed to tire the ex-Marine out. That was definitely a good thing.

"What are you doing?" Gordon asked groggily.

"Watching you," Mario told him.

"What time is it?" Gordon shifted away and began to get up without waiting for an answer. Mario glanced at the clock but didn't answer, getting out of bed as well. They both knew it was time to get their day started. "What happened last night?" Gordon asked, and Mario pulled on his underwear before pausing.

"I don't know… what do you think happened?"

"I'm not sure. But things feel different," Gordon said, and Mario wondered just how much it took him to admit that.

"Different how?" Mario asked, keeping a smirk off his face.

Gordon stood naked near the bed, but the expression on his face made him look stripped bare in other ways as well. "You're not going to make this easy," Gordon said.

"Nope. If you feel different, then you need to tell me, or at least try to describe what you're feeling. Contrary to what you may think, I can't read your mind, and I don't know what you feel unless you tell me, any more than you know what I feel." Mario purposely didn't say anything about his own feelings. After all, Gordon had brought this subject up.

"I think I… God, I don't know. I think that maybe…."

Mario let his smirk show. "Man up, Marine," he told Gordon, and he saw his jaw square as he stood just a bit taller. "The world isn't going to stop if you say what you feel, and maybe I need to hear it. Maybe you need to hear how I feel, but you won't until you open up." Mario paused and stared at Gordon. One way or another, he was going to get this man to say the words.

"I think I may love you," Gordon said, and Mario continued staring. No one wanted that kind of declaration. It was somewhat akin to "I think I may have herpes" on the scale of passion. "Okay, I love you," Gordon said, and Mario instantly moved closer.

"Was that so hard? Because I love you too," Mario whispered, leaning his head against Gordon's ample chest.

"How can you? David just came back, and you were…," Gordon began, but Mario cut him off with a kiss.

"David coming back helped me realize I was carrying a torch for a person and a time that no longer exist. David's the past, but I think you may be the future."

"How do you know?" Gordon asked, and Mario held him a little tighter, for his own reassurance as well as Gordon's.

"I don't. I'm going on what my gut tells me. What does yours say?" Mario asked, and he quickly found himself lifted off his feet and deposited on the bed. The underwear he'd managed to put on was quickly pulled off, and very soon they were joined together with Gordon staring deeply into his eyes, their bodies moving together in a new and exciting rhythm. Mario realized just how long it had been since he'd felt this connection with anyone, and he also realized he hadn't had it with David for a while before he'd left. Gordon touched the spot deep inside him, and all thoughts of anything other than his lover left his mind. For the next half hour, it was as though the world beyond their room didn't exist.

They were definitely a little late for work that morning, but no one said anything. Gordon went right to the barn, while Mario headed to the house to meet with Haven and Dakota. They had plans to make for the next week. Of course both men shared looks back and forth as to the reason why he'd been delayed.

"We have got to do something about these eco people. I had them at my place last night. The dogs woke half the ranch, but I know it was them," Haven said earnestly. "They tried to get into the barn and paddocks. These guys are getting nutty. What do they think, if they let the horses go, they're going to turn back into wild mustangs or something?" Even though it was no laughing matter, Dakota and Mario couldn't help chuckling lightly.

"They're obviously either recruiting people or they're doing their own dirty work now," Dakota said.

"I understand Gordon might have an idea," Haven said, and Mario nodded.

"He mentioned something about that yesterday," Mario offered. "I think he wants David to infiltrate them somehow, but he didn't give too many details." Mario looked away.

"I know. You were a little busy with other things," Haven teased. "Go get him. We need to figure out something sooner rather than later, or these people will cause real damage to us or someone else."

Mario went and found Gordon in the barn, asking him to come to the ranch house. On their way, they passed David and Gordon asked him to come along.

"So what's this plan?" Dakota asked once they were all seated around the kitchen table with mugs of coffee.

"What plan?" David asked, and Haven took a few minutes to fill David in on exactly what had been happening. "And you're going to take advice from him?" David asked, looking at Gordon. "He's the one who started all this."

"David, back off," Mario said a little more sharply than he intended. "He didn't start this, but he might be able to help end it." His conversation with David the day before had settled a lot of things in Mario's mind, and he'd thought that things had been settled for David as well, but apparently not. He should have expected some resentment on David's part, and maybe involving him in whatever Gordon had planned wasn't a good idea.

"Are you sure he isn't here to sabotage you and isn't still working for them?" David asked Dakota. Mario expected Gordon to say something or at the very least give David one of his Marine stares or growls, but he remained quiet and relaxed, which pleased Mario to no end.

"Gordon made a mistake and has more than made up for it. He didn't cause any harm, and if he'd had all the facts, he wouldn't have fallen in with them in the first place. I think the people they're recruiting believe they're trying to help." Dakota shifted his gaze to Gordon. "He's here to help. I believe that. If you don't, then I suggest you leave now. You're good at that, after all." Mario didn't react to Dakota's dig, but he saw David wince. "So what's your decision?"

David didn't move or say anything for quite a while, and Mario thought for sure he was going to leave. "I'll help any way I can," David said.

"Okay," Dakota said and turned to Gordon. "What's your plan?"

"The group seems to recruit people who are a bit desperate and willing to believe what they're saying. They're convincing—after all, they convinced me." Dakota nodded, and Gordon looked at everyone. "I met them at Nancy's Diner on the edge of town, and so did the people who got to the empty cages. They must be using that as a base, or at least a regular hangout."

"How do we know they still use it?" Dakota asked, and Haven shrugged.

"We don't. But they've had luck there in the past, so they may still be using the place. Who knows, the owner may even be involved." Gordon paused. "My idea is to find someone who's new in town, and David, I thought of you. You've been gone for a while, and we would dress you up in old, really scruffy clothes. Make you look like you haven't taken care of yourself. Old backpack, excessively worn jeans, etcetera. Make you look the part," Gordon said.

"What do I do?" David asked.

"Like I said, we'll dress you for the part and you start hanging out at the diner. You don't eat much and always pay with change and ones, no large bills. You need to look desperate and wait to see if they contact you. When they do, you agree to meet them again, and we'll make sure they're met by the sheriff."

"That's it?" David said. "That's all I need to do?"

"That should be all. We're not trying to catch them ourselves—that's the sheriff's job. All we're trying to do is get them to show themselves again so the sheriff can move in. This is a small town and everyone knows everyone else. None of the sheriff's men will work—they're all too well known," Gordon explained, and Mario loved how calm and in charge he sounded. "We'll need to find clothes and things for you. I have an old backpack you can use." Gordon turned to Dakota and Haven. "I need one of you to see if you can round up a PETA sticker. That will silently advertise David's sympathy to the group. They'll look for things like that." Gordon looked at all of them. "Any questions?"

David looked a little uncomfortable. "When do we start?"

"The sooner the better. If they recruit you, we have a chance to put them out of action. If they recruit someone else, then either

Wally's animals or one of the other ranchers is in jeopardy. We need to get everything together, but that shouldn't take too long."

"What if I get in trouble?" David asked.

"I won't be far away. You won't see me, and neither will anyone else, but I'll be there," Gordon said confidently. Mario could tell from the excitement in his voice that Gordon's Marine training was kicking in. "The most important thing for you is to look and act like you're down on your luck. Those seem to be the kind of people they recruit. They don't seem to do their dirty work themselves, so I suspect we may be a bit shocked when we discover who these people are." Gordon stared at David. "Are you really up for this? I know you agreed, but you don't have to do this." Gordon looked at everyone around the table. "None of us will think any less of you if you don't."

David looked at him and Mario like he was expecting some answer from him, but he had none to give.

"Think about it," Gordon said, and David nodded but said nothing. Gordon once again looked at everyone and then stood up. "If there's nothing more, I have some things to do." Gordon left the kitchen, and Mario heard the front door close a few seconds later. Haven, Dakota, David, and he all looked at each other.

"I think it's our best shot," Haven said. "We've gotta stop these people, and the sheriff is a great guy, but stuff like this isn't what he's used to dealing with."

"I agree. David, are you up for this?" Dakota asked, and he nodded

"I think so," he answered. Just then Dakota's phone went off. He answered it and then excused himself, hurrying out of the house. Haven excused himself as well, and then it was only Mario and David.

"So what's really bothering you?" Mario asked David as he got up to refill his coffee mug.

David sighed. "It's really over between us, isn't it?" David put up his hand before Mario could answer. "I really was hoping we could start again. I made the biggest mistake of my life when I left."

"We talked about this yesterday, and I thought you understood. I waited for you for a long time. I kept hoping you would come back, but I now know it was over between us for a while before you left. We were growing apart," Mario said, sitting back down at the table. "That's the reason you followed the job and that other guy to Montana, I know that now."

David turned in the direction of the barn. "But *him*? You really like him?" David asked, and Mario knew he was referring to Gordon.

"Yes, I do," Mario answered, a slight smile forming on his lips. "I think I've earned some happiness, and as much as it may pain you, I think you should be happy for me. We can't go back, and I hope you find someone who makes you happy, but it's not going to be me, not anymore." Mario lightly took David's hand, squeezing it once before letting go. He picked up his mug and stood up from the table. "I think we all have work to do."

David nodded slowly and stood up as well. Together, they left the house. Haven was outside talking to one of the hands, and as soon as he saw David, he motioned him over. They both got in Haven's truck and then they headed away. Mario watched them and breathed a sigh of relief before looking for Gordon. He expected to find him in the barn, but found him in the house on the phone.

"Can you send that right away?" He was smiling as he listened to whoever was on the other end of the line. "I'll look for it tomorrow. Thanks. I owe you one, Greeves." More laughter followed, and then Gordon rattled off the address of the ranch. He talked for a few minutes more, probably Marine-buddy stuff before ending the call. Mario didn't really listen, wanting to give Gordon some privacy.

"One of your buddies?" Mario asked, and Gordon hummed his answer, already heading down the hall to his room. Mario didn't follow, figuring he didn't need to meddle in what Gordon was doing.

"I have some things I'm going to try," Gordon said, and Mario followed his voice. In the bedroom, Gordon had pulled out an old knapsack. "This should work, and we can fill it with various crap to make David look authentic. My buddy Greeves is in Norfolk, and he's going to send me some surveillance gear. I'm going to bug the knapsack so I can hear what's going on, in case David gets in trouble." Gordon was still looking through the closet. "Here they are," Gordon said and pulled out an old pair of jeans. "These will be perfect."

"They're way too big for David," Mario said.

"That's the point. Desperate people don't have proper clothes. They've usually lost weight from skipping meals or getting what they can from charity. That doesn't lend itself to a good fit. Come to think of it, we have to tell David not to shower for a few days. He shouldn't be rank, but he shouldn't smell like soap either."

"How do you know all this?" Mario asked.

"Camouflage is more than just wearing the multicolored uniforms. It's blending into your surroundings so no one sees you. That often means looking like a native. I can wear a turban or a kaffiyeh, and we once had one of the smaller men dress up in a burqa. It's all about watching people and acting the same way they do, especially when you're trying to find out information." Gordon went back to digging and came up with a few more things, then shoved them into the knapsack.

"Do you really think David can do this?" Mario asked. "Couldn't you change your appearance enough that you could do it yourself? Not that I want you in harm's way, but I know you can take care of yourself better than David."

Gordon shrugged. "Maybe, but the haircut would be a dead giveaway, as would the fact that I'm as big as I am. I tend to be memorable, and with as many failed attempts as they've had without being caught, I think whoever is behind this is being very careful.

We could probably use one of the hands, but they're all pretty well known. I think it's probably David or we scrap the plan all together."

"We could secure things here," Mario said. He didn't doubt that Gordon could do what he said he could do, but he was concerned about putting either him or David in harm's way.

Gordon stopped his rummaging and turned toward him. "Yes, we could, but the best defense is a good offense. I don't think these people are going to stop until they accomplish what they set out to do. They were pretty fanatical when they approached me, and they truly believe what they're saying. I think that was what convinced me to go along with them. There's no deception in them, because they believe what they're saying, even though it's wrong. And you know what will happen if one of Wally's cats gets out: we'll have to hunt it and kill it. Then the county will shut Wally down and take away all the cats. We know how hard it is to find homes for them, so all of them will be euthanized in the name of public safety."

"That would kill Wally," Mario said, knowing how much Wally cared for all the animals on the ranch. "I've seen him sit up all night with a sick calf or foal."

"I know, so we have to give this a try." Gordon stopped what he was doing and moved closer. "We're going to be fine." Gordon lightly touched his shoulders. "This isn't going to be particularly dangerous. We don't have to confront them, only inform the sheriff if they make contact, and there's no guarantee they will. This could be a complete waste of time, but I think we have to try. Before we start, we'll arrange a timeline, and if nothing happens in a few days, we'll pack it in and try something else." Gordon smiled wickedly. "I'm thinking landmines around the perimeter, and I can see if the Navy has any extra smart bombs they aren't using."

Mario playfully punched Gordon's shoulder. "I just want these people gone. The entire ranch is on edge, and the hands keep looking over their shoulders. Haven told me he was working with Jeremy and the ATV backfired because he shut it down too fast, and

Jeremy hit the dirt. Even though no guns have been involved, everyone is jittery and worried. No one likes to think of people sneaking around your home."

"Then for now, this is the best idea I have," Gordon said. "Trust me, I have no intention of getting anyone hurt." Mario knew that, but he still couldn't help worrying. "Is this about David?"

"Yes and no," Mario answered honestly, and Gordon scowled slightly. "Just because he and I are no longer together doesn't mean I don't still care about what happens to him. There's no need for you to act jealous. And for the record, I'm worried about you too." Mario lightly kissed him and then moved away, because if they stayed close, he knew they would get involved in other things and there was most definitely still work to be done. But Gordon had other ideas and tugged him close, the heat from beneath Gordon's clothes reaching Mario's skin.

"I know what I'm doing, and I'll do everything I can to keep both of us safe," Gordon said before kissing Mario's breath away. "Now I better finish this up, and you need to go back to work, or I'm going to throw you on the bed and everyone on the ranch is going to know what we're doing by your screams."

Mario gasped and swallowed hard, reluctantly moving away from Gordon. "I'll see you outside," Mario rasped with a very dry mouth and left the room, heading outside to see what was happening and what still needed to be done. Mario found himself keeping an eye on the house until he saw Gordon exit and return to the barn to get to work. Mario worried, and he couldn't help it—he didn't want anything to happen to David or Gordon. He understood that Gordon knew what he was doing and had experience with this type of thing, but he didn't want him in harm's way. He didn't want anyone in harm's way, but he couldn't think of a better alternative.

THAT evening, they sat around Wally and Dakota's kitchen table. Gordon handed David the pants and shirt he'd found, along with a worn, long belt that had definitely seen better days. "Go try this stuff on and we'll see how it looks," Gordon told David, who took the clothes, looking dubious, and left the room.

"Do you really think this is going to work?" Wally asked once David was out of the room.

"I don't know," Gordon answered with a shrug. "I know that the diner is where they contacted me and the guys who came after me. Since we all failed, they may be looking someplace else, but that diner seems to be the place where the seedier types in town tend to hang out. If it doesn't work, we aren't out anything except a few late nights. If it works, we have a chance of catching these guys," Gordon said, fidgeting with the pack he'd brought.

David returned, swimming a bit in the clothes. "These won't work," David said, already tugging on the pants, the legs extending past his feet.

"They're perfect. Roll up the pant legs and tighten the belt," Gordon instructed. "Remember, you're not a bum, just a guy who is a bit down on his luck and trying to make do. Tuck in the shirt and try to make it look as good as possible." Gordon handed him the knapsack. "Throw this over one arm." David complied and Gordon looked him over. "Do you have really old shoes?"

"Yeah," David said.

"Then wear those with work socks. You may think no one will see them, but the smallest detail will give you away. We're going to start tomorrow evening, so wear those clothes for part of the day tomorrow while you're working. They shouldn't look fresh or smell laundry clean."

"I got the PETA sticker," Wally said before reaching behind him to retrieve it off the counter. Gordon took it and handed it to Mario. "Rough it up and rub it in the dirt a bit. We want everything to look old and worn."

Mario took the sticker outside into the twilight and rubbed it into the soil near the edge of the drive, making sure to scratch it on some rocks. He also folded and crumpled it multiple times before taking it back inside.

"Are you still sure you can do this?" Dakota was asking David. "You know you don't have to."

"I know. But I helped Wally build those first enclosures and took care of the cats for him sometimes," David said as Mario returned to the kitchen and handed Gordon the sticker. "I missed this place when I was gone."

"Okay," Dakota said, turning to Gordon, who attached the sticker to the side of the knapsack.

"Should I have a phone?" David asked, and Gordon thought for a few minutes.

"Okay, but only use it in an emergency and keep it hidden. A cell phone is probably something you would have given up. We'll need to make sure it's an old one," Gordon said. "Okay. You're not to be a hero. If you see any sign that things aren't going well or you feel uncomfortable, get up and leave. Go right to your car and get the hell out of there, understood?" Gordon asked firmly.

"Yes."

"Good. Watch the people in the restaurant, but don't appear to be watching them. They may be involved," Gordon explained, and again David agreed. "Now, when you arrive, take a corner table if possible, but sit near a window so I can see you. Be polite. Not too friendly, but approachable. Say thank you to the server when she brings your coffee, and when it arrives put lots of sugar in it. The packets are free and sugar is energy."

"I hate my coffee that way," David said.

"Now you love it. As I was saying, order something basic and pay with change or ones and make a bit of a show about fishing for the money. You have it, but you need to find it, and be sure to leave a tip for the waitress. Once you're done eating, pull out a newspaper that's a few days old and spread it on the table, like you're reading it. It's hot right now and the diner is air-conditioned." Gordon reached over and ruffled David's hair. "That's better. Don't have your hair perfect—make it look like you combed it with your fingers."

"Is there anything else I should do?" David asked.

"Nope. Just hope they make contact. You should look like a good target. If they do make contact, act wary, but you're a bit desperate. And they will probably offer you money, which you find hard to turn down. Act skeptical, but fairly easy to convince. Once they make contact, fold the paper and put it away. If someone approaches you and you don't think it's them, leave the paper spread on the table. When you feel you can't linger any longer, get up, throw the paper away, and leave the diner. It's that simple."

"Okay," David said.

"The important thing," Gordon added sternly, "is if someone joins you at the table and you fold the paper, I'll call the sheriff. Got it?"

"Yeah," David said a bit testily.

"He's doing this to protect you," Mario told David, and some of the tension slipped from David's body.

"When you're there, act as relaxed as possible. I know you'll be nervous, but try not to look it. You aren't there for anything other than a meal and a chance to cool down. Then you'll be on your way. If anyone asks why you're in town, say you're looking for work. You used to live here, but left and are hoping to find a job. Stay close to the truth without giving details. It'll most likely be chatter just to make conversation, but you never know."

"So that's it?" David asked.

"Yep," Gordon said.

"Can I change out of these clothes?" David asked, and Gordon chuckled lightly.

"Of course," Gordon said. "And for the record, it takes guts to do what you're doing." David looked over his shoulder, probably to see if Gordon was joking, but Mario knew he wasn't. He very much doubted Gordon ever joked about things like courage and honor. David seemed to realize it too, because he smiled slightly and then left the room, walking just a little taller.

"So what do the rest of us do?" Wally asked once David had left.

"Stay away and go about things normally here. Watch over your cats and make sure no one gets to them," Gordon said. "Let David and me handle this end of the operation while you make sure the ranch keeps going." Mario nearly laughed, but kept it to himself somehow. Wally rarely stayed home and seldom kept to himself, and he could already see Wally's mind churning. So could Gordon, apparently. "Don't think about showing up there," Gordon said, narrowing his eyes. Dakota pulled Wally to him with a grin.

"Don't worry, I'll keep him busy," Dakota said, pulling the smaller man onto his lap. Dakota whispered something into Wally's ear, and Mario saw him blush, big-time.

"I think we all need to make an early night of it. Tomorrow promises to be a long day for all of us." Gordon stood up, and Mario did as well. "I know all of you are going to be excited, but I want to caution everyone that this isn't a game, and we may come up empty-handed. I'm willing to try for a few nights, but we can't do this long term. We'd all be too tired to run the ranch, and that's more important."

Wally, Dakota, and Haven nodded their agreement. As they got ready to leave, Phillip came in the door. "Is something wrong?" Haven asked, looking like he was ready to bolt into action.

"No. I was just trying to find you," Phillip said softly.

"I was just heading home," Haven said. David rejoined them, carrying a neatly folded pile of clothes. Haven handed David a set of keys, and they left together. "We'll be along in a little while," Haven told David as they left. The last thing Mario heard was a deep almost giggle from Phillip.

"We should be going too," Mario said as he took Gordon's hand and led him outside as well. It definitely seemed like the kind of night for love. The moon hung huge in the sky, and the horses and soft sounds of the cattle lowing drifted over the land, all of it to the accompaniment of crickets. For a few seconds, Mario thought about grabbing some blankets and finding a secluded spot for them to be alone outside, but thought better of it. As attractive as that sounded, a comfortable bed held more appeal, so he led Gordon toward the house.

"Where were Haven and Phillip going that had Phillip giggling like that?" Gordon asked, and Mario stopped. Maybe he should rethink the outdoor notion.

"There's a rise on the edge of one of the ranges close to Haven and Phillip's spread. It's a great spot to look up at the stars, and I've seen Haven's truck parked up there a number of times. It seems to be sort of a special spot for him and Phillip, although I don't know why. And I don't intend to ask." They stopped walking, and Gordon gravitated toward the paddocks.

"I love watching the colt," Gordon said softly in the near darkness, the light from the barn indirectly illuminating the area. "He's so innocent and unspoiled by life." Gordon turned to Mario. "Sometimes I feel so messed up, and other times, like tonight, I'm on top of my game and know exactly what I'm doing." Gordon turned back to the colt, both he and his mother horse-shaped black spots in a field of dark gray that faded to inky blackness. "I was there and I can't remember a thing. I should have been better than that. I was trained to watch all around me, to remember details most people never even see, and yet part of the day that meant life and death for my best friends, hell, *family*, I can't remember."

"Have you ever thought that you simply can't access it?" Mario asked, and he saw Gordon turn toward him again. "Your brain may have recorded everything, but it's walled it off and isn't letting you get to it."

"That's what the shrink said, and when I asked him how I could get to it, he just shrugged and said maybe someday something would trigger the pathway to it. He also said I may never remember. A lot of help he was." Gordon put an arm around his waist, turning back to the paddock. "I tried hypnotism a few times, but they couldn't reach it either. The one thing everyone I saw confirmed was that someday I may remember, but then again I may not."

"I know you're afraid that if you do remember, you'll realize you did something wrong, but that's only part of it, isn't it?" Mario asked.

"Yeah. Stacks's and Bottles's families deserve to know exactly what happened. The other guys in the patrol have pieced together part of what happened, but so many of them were injured and out of it that details are spotty, and none of them saw what happened to Bottles and Stacks, so their families only have guesses and conjecture. No real answers." Gordon tapped the side of his head with his free hand. "It may be all locked up here"—he slapped his temple—"but it isn't letting go." Gordon sighed and grew silent. Eventually the colt wandered over, nuzzling Gordon's shirt for a treat.

"You're going to spoil him," Mario teased.

"Not possible. He should know happiness and innocence for as long as possible," Gordon said, patting the colt's neck lightly before turning away.

"Come on, big guy," Mario said with a smile that Gordon probably couldn't see. "I'll take you inside. I can't do anything about your innocence, that's probably long gone, but I can spoil you."

Gordon chuckled at first, and then it built into a full-on laugh. Mario listened to the joyful sound and realized he hadn't heard it before, at least not like that. Before he realized what was happening, Gordon raced at him. Gordon lifted Mario off his feet and slung him over his shoulder. "What are you doing?" Mario gasped and began to laugh himself. Gordon moved toward the house. "Put me down," he said through continued laughter as he bounced with each of Gordon's steps. "Gordon," Mario cried through chuckles until he realized he was in a perfect position and grabbed Gordon's butt.

Gordon squeaked, and that made Mario laugh even harder. Mario never thought he'd live to hear a Marine squeal like a girl, but... he continued laughing and slid his hand inside Gordon's pants. That got him a gasp of surprise. Mario heard Gordon open the door, and then Gordon carried him inside. Gordon kicked the door closed and then strode down the hallway before depositing him on the bed with a bounce. "You're bad," Gordon teased.

"And you're a caveman," Mario retorted, but he lost his train of thought as Gordon stripped off his shirt and began opening his pants. Very soon his Marine was a naked caveman Marine, and Mario didn't give a damn about anything other than the way Gordon stripped him bare before joining him on the bed. "But you're my caveman," Mario added before yanking Gordon into a kiss. Their bodies vibrated together as they kissed, Mario sliding his throbbing cock along Gordon's smooth skin. He moaned softly and then louder when he felt Gordon moving against him.

Gordon broke their kiss, latching onto a nipple and sucking hard enough that Mario arched his back, mashing his chest to Gordon's face.

"Oh, God yes!" Mario cried, and Gordon sucked harder before transferring his lips to the other bud, lavishing it with equal attention. "Jesus," Mario said, catching his breath as Gordon moved his lips away from his skin. Before he could say anything, Gordon flipped him onto his stomach, and then he settled between Mario's splayed legs. Gordon ran his hands up Mario's calves and then thighs, spreading his legs further. Hot breath blew over his skin, and Mario clutched the pillow as the warm air was followed by searing hot lips and tongue.

He threw his head back, opening his mouth in a silent cry as Gordon slid his tongue over Mario's opening. The breath he'd managed to catch after their kissing was lost again and he gasped ineffectually when Gordon licked and teased him to distraction. All he could do was try to get enough air in his lungs and clutch his pillow as Gordon rimmed him stupid.

Mario shook, shivered, whined, and moaned as Gordon tongue-fucked him deep and hard. Then, just when he could feel the first tingles that told him his climax was building, Gordon stopped. Mario felt as though he were hanging in midair.

Gordon slowly breached him with a thick finger, locating the spot inside him, and soon Mario vibrated again. One finger turned to two, and Mario gasped at the stretch. Gordon slipped his fingers away, and Mario felt the bed shift. A tear, a snick, and then he was rolled onto his back, heels on Gordon's shoulders. Gordon entered him hard and fast—they were both too far gone for anything else.

Mario locked his gaze on Gordon's as their bodies slammed together over and over, Mario taking whatever Gordon had to give. Their frantic coupling couldn't last long. Mario was already so primed that as soon as he felt the slightest irregularity in Gordon's movements, he stroked himself hard and fast, coming within seconds, with Gordon right behind him. Gordon collapsed onto him. Mario held him, and he was held in return as they caught their breath. Without thinking, Mario closed his eyes, listening to Gordon's breathing. "I don't like you doing this," Mario said softly. "I hate the thought of you in danger."

"I know," Gordon replied, hugging Mario tighter.

"We have to try, but I don't have to like it."

"I know that too," Gordon said. "Everything will be all right."

Mario nodded, opening his eyes again and watching as Gordon left the room, returning a minute later with a cloth. He never stopped watching him, and once Gordon returned from the bathroom, he climbed in bed and held him tight. Mario couldn't help feeling that this could be the last time they were like this. Mario knew it was probably his imagination. What they were planning was mostly to watch, find the guys causing the problems, and call the sheriff. He knew that, but he couldn't seem to shake the concern settling deep in his stomach.

"It's going to be fine. I've done things like this plenty of times and in places much more dangerous than here," Gordon said, shifting a bit closer. Mario knew he was trying to reassure him, but it wasn't helping. He was still nervous and worried. Quietly, he hoped nothing happened and that David sat there for however many days they decided to do this, waiting for something that didn't happen. "I know you don't want anyone in harm's way, but we have to try."

"I know," Mario said as he lightly stroked Gordon's bicep. "We have to try to put an end to this, and I know you're the best person for the job. You'll keep David safe, but my real concern is who is going to make sure you're safe."

Gordon chuckled very softly. "I can take care of myself. That isn't something you need to worry about." Gordon kissed him lightly. "Go to sleep. We're all going to need all the rest we can get." Mario nodded and closed his eyes, hoping that sleep would come and it did… eventually.

Chapter Nine

GORDON lay on his belly surrounded by tall grass and scrub, dressed in camouflage with branches attached to his hat. There was no way anyone who wasn't specifically looking for him could see him, and even then it was doubtful he could be seen. Slowly, he lifted the night vision goggles Greeves had sent along with the listening gear and scanned the area around the diner to see if anyone approached other than by the conventional methods. There hadn't been any movement in the surrounding scrub other than a deer that wandered close enough to be seen and then skittered away at the sound of an approaching car. He was really beginning to think this might be a fool's errand. Nothing about the diner looked out of the ordinary and hadn't all night, or last night, for that matter.

"Would you like a refill on your coffee?" the waitress asked David, who said he would. Through the window, Gordon watched her pour from the pot and then leave the table. He really wished he could have found a spot closer than across the street, but he needed to stay hidden. There was no cover any closer, and he was here primarily to make sure David was okay.

Yesterday, nothing had happened at all. David had entered the diner and sat down at a window table. There had only been one left when he arrived, and Gordon had hoped no one would take it before David got there. He ordered coffee and then a bit of food, ate it all, and opened his paper to read, just like they planned. Nothing happened. No one other than the waitress approached him all night, and after an hour and a half, David asked the waitress where he could get a cheap place for the night. She pointed him to the motel up the street. "She looked like she didn't believe I had the money for that," David had said once they got back to the ranch—the exact impression they wanted to give.

One thing Gordon did notice was that he didn't see the server for a while after David left, but then she was back. Gordon waited to see if anything else happened or if any of the people who'd approached him showed up, but after an hour, the diner looked completely normal and Gordon had lost his ears inside, so he packed it in.

Things seemed to be going the same way tonight. The waitress remembered David and seemed a little chattier as she brought his food. Gordon's ears perked up when she remarked on the PETA sticker on his bag, but then she left and David slowly ate what he'd ordered. Gordon remembered the waitress from when he'd eaten at the diner, but at the time he hadn't paid much attention to her.

"More coffee?" she asked when she returned with the pot, and Gordon noticed that she was paying more attention to David than she had the night before. She poured the coffee, and Gordon saw her linger a few seconds without saying anything before moving away again. Things definitely had a different feel from last night.

David finished eating and spread out his paper. The server returned again, filling up his mug. David added a bit of sugar, then stirred the coffee. The waitress hadn't moved. "Do you need anything else?" she asked, moving her hips slightly, and Gordon pursed his lips to keep from laughing. Oh God, she was coming on to David. "I have some things that are much better than coffee." Gordon stopped himself from laughing. This was more serious than that.

"No, thank you," David said with more brightness than Gordon could have managed, even though Gordon heard David's nervousness underneath. "I'm good." Once the waitress left the table, David got up, leaving his paper and mug, and headed to the bathroom. Thankfully, he was carrying the knapsack. "Jesus," he said softly once the door closed. Gordon heard water running and figured David was splashing water over his face. Gordon heard a towel dispenser snap while he watched David's table. No one approached, but Gordon was ready to hurry in and get David out if anyone tried to put something in David's mug.

Once David returned, Gordon watched him and the server who approached another table, pulling something out of her cleavage. Money changed hands fast, and the goods were back in the boobage fast enough that Gordon nearly missed it. He knew they were pills, from what David was whispering, and Gordon started to wonder if he should pull David out, call the sheriff with what he'd seen, and get both of them the hell out of there.

Gordon zoomed in on him. David knew he was out there watching, and Gordon had explained what he could see, so he saw David turn to look out the window. Hopefully the others would think he was staring into the darkness, but Gordon saw the worried but resolute expression on his face. Gordon didn't like what he'd seen, and after thinking about it some more, he'd decided to get David out of there when two cars he thought might be familiar pulled into the lot. This could be it.

Three guys got out, but he couldn't see their faces clearly even with the night vision. They were just far enough away that he could see their outlines, but not enough detail. He waited until they entered the diner and sat in a booth near David. None of them seemed to be paying any attention to anything around them. Gordon had pulled out his phone, ready to call David and get him out, when one of the men stood up and walked back to the bathroom. The man paused briefly at David's table and then continued on past and out of view.

His heart sped up as he waited. He heard David turn the page of the newspaper and saw him glance toward the bathroom. He clearly thought this was the guy as well. All Gordon needed was someone to try to contact David and then he'd call the police.

The man walked back out, and Gordon got a good look at him. He wasn't someone Gordon recognized, and he wished the others would move so he could see them better. They'd taken a table away from the window, and he was unable to make them out in any detail. A few more cars pulled up, and Gordon shifted his gaze. He suppressed a whistle when he saw two men getting out of a top-of-the-line Cadillac. They strode into the diner, and Gordon saw them speaking directly with the waitress. She moved out of his sight, but Gordon knew what was going on. "Damn," he swore under his breath. His little operation to see if they could identify the eco people bent on getting to Wally's animals had put David in the middle of some sort of drug deal.

Gordon twisted in the grass and pulled out his phone. He'd placed tape over the display so he didn't get any light. He was about to make a call to the sheriff when the phone vibrated in his hand. He knew he should ignore it, but took the call anyway. "What," he whispered.

"Is everything okay?" Mario asked.

"No, call the sheriff now," Gordon whispered as he lifted the glasses and saw a man sit across from David in the booth. It was one of the men who had talked to him. "Tell him we have the eco people and that there's a drug deal going down." Gordon hung up the phone and thought about calling the sheriff himself.

"I've been a PETA member for years," David said, and Gordon remembered to pay attention to the mic. "Worked with animals in Montana until I disagreed with the ranch owner about how he was treating his horses. Bastard canned me," David was saying, and Gordon marveled as David said exactly the right thing. Part of Gordon wanted David out of there and part of him wanted David to stall for time. "Ranchers think they know best, and yet most of them don't really give a damn about how they treat their animals as long as they do the work they want," David added.

"You're so right," the other man said. "There is a ranch here where they keep animals in cages. They don't feed them or water them properly." Gordon knew that voice, and knowing he was talking about Wally made Gordon's blood boil. He'd believed that crap once, but he knew it wasn't true now and wanted to wring the fucker's neck. "We've been trying to get them to listen and take better care of them, but they won't." He sounded so passionate and convinced that he was right, even though Gordon knew he was full of shit. "So now we're forced to take action," he said softly but with the force of passion.

"What sort of action?" David asked with equal passion, and Gordon thought he might mean it for a few seconds.

"We have been trying to teach them a lesson and free those animals, but up till now we haven't had any luck," he added in a whisper that Gordon strained to hear, but it was enough. These were the people they had been looking for, and now all he needed to do was figure a way to get David out of there. Still watching, he saw David close the newspaper and slowly stand up.

"I have to be going," David said and turned to leave the restaurant. The man grabbed David's arm, and Gordon nearly leapt from where he'd been hiding. Unfortunately, he heard more shuffling of the knapsack than what was actually being said. But then David moved away as Gordon heard sirens approach. He disappeared from sight, and Gordon waited until David reached the door of the diner before breathing again. The sirens got louder and police cars began pulling into the diner parking lot.

David moved toward his car and stopped as deputies began filing out of their cars. David was about to pull open the door to his car when all hell broke loose. Shots rang out from inside the diner, and Gordon saw David go down as those shots were answered. Men took up positions behind their vehicles as others from inside the diner rushed out a side door, eager to escape. Gordon paid no attention to them or anything else. In a near rage and rush of energy, he was up and across the street in a matter of seconds. Before anyone could stop him, he was at David's side. Shots rang out again and then all was silent.

Gordon bent to where David lay slumped on the ground. As he lifted David up, he felt blood on David's clothes. Without thinking, he carried David to one of the sheriff's vehicles. "I need to get this man to a hospital," Gordon said, already reaching to pull open the door.

"Who are you and where did you come from?"

"I'm the man who had you called, and there's no time. I'll answer all your questions on the way, but we must get him to the hospital now." Gordon didn't wait. He set David on the seat and climbed in after him. "Now, you fool!" he barked in his best drill-sergeant voice. "Let's move!"

Within seconds, the deputy closed the door, and after a few seconds, he saw the sheriff peer into the window and then nod to the deputy, who got in front. The car began to move, and Gordon began searching David for his injury. He found it just below his left shoulder. Applying pressure, he did his best to staunch the bleeding while the siren wailed into the night.

"Who are you?" asked the deputy.

"Gordon Fisher," he answered without looking away from David. "We were watching the diner to catch the guys who keep recruiting people to set the cats free on the ranch. By the way, they were in the diner." Gordon described them, and the officer relayed the descriptions over the radio. "You can also tell the sheriff that I saw the big-boobed waitress selling out of her cleavage. She has a bag of what I guess are pills stuffed in there."

The officer relayed the information. "Where were you watching from?"

"Across the street," Gordon said, grateful that the bleeding seemed to have stopped, at least for now. "I had night-vision binoculars. In case you couldn't guess, I'm a Marine."

The deputy chuckled. "I sort of figured. My dad was in the Corps, and you sounded just like him."

The radio cackled, and Gordon heard the calls but didn't pay too much attention. "You're going to be fine, David. It isn't too bad, and they'll be able to help you at the hospital." Gordon felt David trying to move. "Stay still. I've got the bleeding stopped, but if you move it'll start again. We're almost there."

The car flew over the roads. "How was he shot?" the officer asked.

"One of the dealers got him," Gordon said. "I'll be happy to tell you everything I saw once we're at the hospital and he's being looked at." Gordon's heart raced at the thought of losing someone else he'd been tasked with protecting.

"They have the three men you described and the waitress in custody. The others aren't in good shape. Luckily, the only innocent person hurt was him," the officer said. "It could have been a lot worse."

Not for Gordon. He'd been charged with protecting David and he'd gotten shot. Gordon knew he should have gotten David out of there as soon as the waitress flashed what was in her bra. He wanted to kick himself for waiting, but he'd seen a chance to accomplish the mission they'd set out to do. He'd wanted to complete their objective. They pulled into the hospital emergency area, sirens still calling, and people rushed out. They carefully lifted David out of the car, and Gordon got a good look at him—shirt covered with blood, face pale and contorted in pain. Gordon pulled out his phone and called Mario.

"We're at the hospital. David was shot," he said, watching as David was placed on a gurney and wheeled inside. Gordon took a single step and then fell back against the car as everything locked away inside his memory opened up and rushed forward.

"Are you okay?" the deputy asked from next to him. "Were you hurt too? I can get someone to help."

"No, I'm fine," Gordon said, but he wasn't fine. His legs didn't want to work as his entire mind was nearly overwhelmed by the rush of memory. "It'll pass soon. Just a flashback." Those were the last words Gordon said before collapsing onto the ground.

The assault on his senses was overwhelming. His ears filled with the sound of gunfire, his eyes with the decimation of the men he knew, and his nose with the scent of blood, panic, and fear. Gordon felt people helping him up and into a chair. "I'm okay," Gordon said feebly, opening his eyes. He was in a wheelchair and being pushed inside the building. "It's just a bit of post-traumatic stress," Gordon explained.

"We still need to check you out," the man said, and Gordon was ready to protest when Mario rushed up to him.

"What happened? Are you hurt?" Mario sounded half panicked.

"I'm fine. David was shot in the shoulder. They already took him inside," Gordon told him. "It seems we ended up in the middle of some sort of drug deal." Gordon turned to the man pushing him. "I need to know if the other man is going to be okay." The doors opened and the orderly pushed Gordon inside.

"I don't know, sir," he said, and he pushed Gordon to a window where a woman sat behind a desk and began asking him questions.

"I'm fine," Gordon said, standing up. "I don't need to be admitted or waste the doctor's time."

"He fainted," said the man who'd wheeled him in.

"I didn't faint," Gordon snapped and then eased his tone before turning to Mario. "I remembered." A tingling feeling began in Gordon's neck and ran down his spine. "I remember everything."

"Oh," Mario said softly. "Do you want to go somewhere and talk about it?"

"Not now. We have to see how David is, and when I can put all the pieces together, I'll tell you what happened. It's a bit jumbled right now, but it's all there." Gordon shivered involuntarily at the thought of having to tell anyone what had happened. Gordon turned back to the woman and said, "Thank you, ma'am, but I'm fine." He stepped away from the window and sat down in one of the waiting room chairs. Mario sat on one side and the deputy on the other. Gordon told him everything he saw and why he'd been watching the diner.

"You should have contacted us," the deputy scolded when Gordon explained his stakeout.

"It wasn't your animals that were in danger, or your ranch they were invading," Gordon told him with carefully controlled anger. "You couldn't find them, so we did." Gordon's anger melted as he thought of David. "What we didn't count on was a drug deal taking place at the same time. We were only going to watch and call you when we were sure it was them."

"I was the one who called you, at Gordon's urging," Mario interjected. The deputy asked a lot of questions to get details of what they'd seen as well as their personal information.

"Are you waiting for Mr. Bricmont?" a doctor asked.

Both Gordon and Mario stood up, as did the deputy. "Yes."

"He's going to be fine. He lost a fair amount of blood, but the bullet missed the bone and passed through the soft tissue, which is why there was so much blood. We're going to keep him here at least overnight," the doctor said.

"Can we see him?" Mario asked, and the doctor nodded. Mario stood up to follow, but Gordon stayed where he was.

"You go, I'll wait here," Gordon said. He somehow doubted David wanted to see him.

Mario followed the doctor, and Gordon took a deep breath, releasing it with a long sigh once Mario was gone.

"It isn't your fault your friend got hurt," the deputy said. "Well, yes, you should have left the surveillance to us, but you didn't shoot him. And once you figured out what was going on, you did the right thing and called us."

"I should have gotten him out of there earlier," Gordon said.

The deputy nodded. "Maybe. But I bet he saw the same things you did, and he didn't leave either. I somehow doubt very much if he holds you to blame." The deputy got up. "I need to check in and relay this information to the sheriff. I'm sure we'll be in touch soon." The deputy looked around and then extended his hand. "They'll kill me for saying this, but you did us a favor. We've been after those dealers for a while, and it looks like we got all of them along with those eco people. Maybe things will calm down for a while." The deputy stepped away and walked toward the back. He spoke with the nurse, and she let him through the doors.

A few minutes later, Mario rejoined him. "The deputy is talking to David," Mario explained as he sat down. "They're moving him to a room, and I told him we'd be up tomorrow to see him. They've given him something to help him sleep, so we may as well head for home. Wally is going to be worried sick and will probably be driving Dakota half up a tree."

"Yeah," Gordon agreed, following Mario out of the waiting area and to his truck.

"Do you want to talk about what you remembered?" Mario asked when they were about halfway to the ranch.

"Not really, but I promise I'll tell you everything soon," Gordon said. He'd been trying to keep the memories at bay, but not letting them slip away in case he forgot again. "I'm still getting snippets and flashes of imagery. It's there but sort of jumbled, like my brain hasn't cataloged it yet."

"Okay," Mario said, and Gordon heard the intense curiosity under the surface. Rather than respond, he simply watched the darkness pass by the windows. He hated that David had gotten hurt. His safety had been Gordon's responsibility, and he'd let both Mario and David down. They turned into the drive and parked. Mario opened his door, but Gordon sat in his seat without moving. Finally, he opened the door and got out. Wally and Dakota came out of the house, followed closely by Haven and Phillip.

"How is he?" Wally asked as he rushed over. "You're both okay, aren't you?"

"Yes," Mario answered. "We're fine. David is in the hospital, but he's going to be fine."

"The sheriff is on his way over," Dakota told them, and Gordon nodded. He'd figured they'd be seeing him fairly soon. He and Mario were ushered back inside, and Wally began to fuss. Coffee, food, and almost endless chatter that continued until Wally placed everything on the table. He also brought a clean shirt, probably one of Dakota's, for Gordon to change into. Gordon left the room and changed in the bathroom, throwing the bloody shirt away before returning to the kitchen, where Wally continued fussing until Dakota pulled Wally to him. "They're okay, and David is going to be fine."

A loud knock sounded on the door, and Haven got up and answered it, returning with the sheriff behind him. "I should throw you in jail," the sheriff began, moving closer to Gordon, who braced, but sat still. Dakota however was on his feet.

"If you'd have done something, we wouldn't have had to do this. We all planned this and agreed to it because you found nothing." Gordon was surprised by Dakota's anger. "He told you, and so did the other people you caught where they were recruiting people, but you did nothing. You couldn't find them. It took Gordon two days. So you damned well didn't look too hard." Dakota stood toe to toe in front of the sheriff. "My father thought you were useless, and I now know he was right. I intend to make sure the voters of this county know just how ineffectual their sheriff is."

"Now hold on," the sheriff blustered, puffing out his chest.

"No, you see here. I was there when Mario made the call. Your people were told about both the eco people and the drug deal, and from what I hear, you went in there guns blazing." Dakota glanced at Gordon, who nodded. In that instant, he realized Dakota was bluffing, but the sheriff didn't catch it. "No wonder David was shot. Furthermore, you were told that Gordon was watching the diner, but you and your people didn't listen. So get off your high horse and realize that they did your job for you." Dakota paused in his tirade, breathing deeply without stepping back.

"Okay," the sheriff said, taking a step back, "there's no need to get nasty."

"Then don't come in my home and act like you know everything. Your folks messed up, and that lies on your shoulders," Dakota said much more calmly. "Now, what is it you need?" Dakota backed away as well, and seemed to realize, as Gordon did, that the situation needed to settle down.

"We have the people from both groups in custody. Some of the dealers were wounded, but they'll survive to reach trial." The sheriff turned to Gordon. "I assume you will be available to testify about what you saw."

"Of course," Gordon said.

"Good. We also found your nest, and I have your equipment in the car, along with David's knapsack. Where did you get this stuff? Wait, don't answer that, I don't want to know," the sheriff said. "We'll give it back to you tomorrow. I assume you need to return it." Gordon nodded. The sheriff looked around the table and didn't see many friendly faces.

"I'll see you out," Wally said, moving around Dakota. The sheriff followed, and once the front door closed firmly behind him, Wally returned. "It's been a tough couple of days for all of us, and tomorrow isn't going to be much easier. The sheriff isn't done and he'll be back. We'll also need to check on David, so I suggest we all hit the hay and try to get some sleep." Wally would brook no argument. Haven and Phillip were the first to leave, with Mario and Gordon following quickly behind them.

"See you tomorrow," Mario called to Haven and Phillip before leading the way past the paddocks to the house. "You had me scared to death," Mario said once he'd closed the door. "Once I called the police, I paced and fretted until I got your call from the hospital."

"I know. But as soon as I hung up, all hell broke loose and I had to help David."

Mario moved closer. "I understand, but you still scared me, especially when I saw them hauling you into the hospital. I saw you covered in blood and thought it was yours. Then I found out you'd collapsed."

"I think the situation with David was what freed the memories that had been locked away. I watched them take him away and suddenly I was back in Iraq and they were taking Bottles and Stacks away. Then it was like a door opened and everything came flooding out all at once and I couldn't stop it. It must have overwhelmed me, and I went down. The next thing I know, I'm being lifted into a chair and taken into the hospital. You know the rest," Gordon said, and Mario moved into his arms.

"It still scared the hell out of me." Mario kissed him hard, and Gordon returned the hug. "So are these things you remembered good or bad?"

Gordon swallowed. "They're horrific," he answered. "I'm still piecing things together, but I can understand why they got locked away." Gordon shuddered and held Mario closer. "In some ways, I wish they still were, because without them, I only had the doubt to live with. Now I don't know if I can ever stop seeing what happened." Gordon took a deep breath and tried to stop the snippets of film that seemed to play in his mind. "I'm wondering how I can live with knowing what actually happened." Gordon held Mario tighter.

"If you need someone to talk with about it, we'll get someone," Mario said. "Not some shrink, but someone who understands," Mario told him. Gordon had no idea who he had in mind, but he doubted anyone could help him but him.

"Okay," Gordon said, relieved that Mario hadn't pushed him to talk about it. He wasn't ready to talk about it and he wasn't sure when he would be, but he knew it had to be soon. This wouldn't stay bottled up for long, and he needed to decide how and when to tell Mario what happened.

"Are you going to call the people from the Navy?"

"Yes. I have to, I know that, but not until I tell you," Gordon said.

"Okay," Mario agreed and continued holding him until his cell phone rang. Mario reached into his pocket without letting go. "Hello," he said and then listened for a few seconds. "That's great news. I'll be sure to tell the others, and we'll be by to see you in the morning. Get some sleep—you sound like the medication they've probably given you is working." Mario listened for a few moments longer and then disconnected. "That was David, and they seem to have given him some good drugs, but he said he thinks he's going to be okay. His shoulder hurts like hell, but they said he'll probably regain most of the use of his arm, and the long-term damage would be minimal. He was getting pretty giggly by the end."

Gordon breathed a sigh of relief. "I—"

Mario stepped away from him. "Don't you dare say it," Mario scolded harshly. "What happened was not your fault and you know it. You didn't shoot David and you didn't force him to go in there. From what you said, you were the one who got him out of the way of further harm." Mario smacked his shoulder. "I bet you were on your way while all the crap was still going on, weren't you?" Mario demanded and Gordon met his gaze. "I knew it. They were still shooting and you were trying to help David." Mario continued glaring at him. "That was heroic, brave, and if you ever do anything that reckless that again, I will whip your Marine ass from here to kingdom come. Do you understand me?" Mario yelled. "I was scared to death that you were going to be hurt. I love you, goddammit, and you better stop this kind of crap." Tears rolled down Mario's cheeks, and Gordon pulled Mario to him, holding him tight even as Mario smacked his chest. "Don't you ever do that again."

"Okay," Gordon agreed. "I promise."

"Good, because I don't want to have to beat the shit out of you, but I will," Mario said, even as the tears kept flowing as Mario folded against his body. Gordon felt the emotion and relief well inside him, but he kept them under control as he moved Mario toward the bedroom.

They reached the bed, and Gordon undressed before pulling off Mario's clothes. Somehow he managed it without breaking his hold on Mario for more than a few seconds. He needed Mario, and within seconds, he realized Mario needed him just as badly. But what started off as nearly frantic quickly settled into something warmer, deeper, and definitely more caring.

"I don't want to lose you," Mario confessed, and Gordon felt his heart open wide.

"I don't want to lose you either," he whispered back, holding Mario tighter.

Chapter Ten

"HOW'S David?" Gordon asked from the other end of the sofa a couple days later.

Mario chuckled. "He's going to be fine. He's helping Haven and Phillip around the house as much as he can one-handed. "

"Good," Gordon said a bit sullenly.

"What is it?"

"Last night I relived the whole thing in my dreams. I keep thinking there's something more I could have done," Gordon explained, moving closer.

"Are you ready to talk about it?" Mario asked, and Gordon nodded slowly.

"I think so." Gordon shifted again, until he was sitting right next to him, and Mario took his hand. "I told you we were patrolling the market. There were shells going off everywhere and gunfire from one of the side walls. We tried to protect people as they screamed and ran everywhere. Some of them got so confused they ran toward the shelling." Gordon paused, and Mario knew he was there in his mind.

"Stay here," Mario said softly. "Stay with me."

Gordon nodded. "We realized we needed to get out and started moving toward the exit. Our plan was to try to come around behind the men at the wall and take them out. They were obviously in league with the people shelling because it was the one area of the market not being hit." Gordon paused and swallowed hard. "I can remember the shooting coming from our right. I headed in the direction we'd indicated and a shell went off right behind us. I was thrown off my feet and toward the side of a building. I must have hit my head because I remember my head hurting and a ringing in my ears. I got up and hurried back to the guys." Gordon gasped hard, and Mario thought he was going to go to pieces, but he steadied himself.

"It's okay. If you aren't up to it, you don't have to tell me," Mario said, the pain on Gordon's face ripping at his heart. He'd known this was going to be difficult for Gordon to talk about, but he'd had no idea how much it would rip at his own heart.

Gordon shook his head hard. "I have to get this out," Gordon said with surprising calmness. "I found the rest of the guys on the ground. There were so many of them that I grabbed Stacks and lifted him over my shoulder. I got him into a building near the edge of the market and hurried back. The fighting seemed concentrated on the other side of the market, so I hoped he was safe. People were still running and trying to get out as I made my way back. Another shell exploded...." Gordon paused and Mario could almost see the concussion rock through Gordon's body the way it must have then. "I hit the ground and then scrambled up. I made it back to the guys. I lifted Bottles onto my shoulder, then I pulled Harper to his feet and led the two of them to the building. Harper was awake, but hurt. I set him on the floor along with Bottles and rushed back." Gordon took a deep breath, then continued. "I was covered in blood, but in the heat it was already drying, making my clothes stiff. From somewhere I heard return fire and managed to make it back again." Gordon shuddered. "An Iraqi was standing over them with a machine gun, and I knew he was about to pull the trigger. Simply reacting, I swung my rifle from my back like a club, connecting with his head. I shot him where he lay and then went back to work. This part is still fuzzy, but the other guys were down, bleeding. I remember being nearly dead on my feet, but I can remember the sensation of tugging men barely able to walk to their feet and somehow getting them back to the building."

Gordon paused again, and Mario sat dumbfounded, unable to speak for a while. He swallowed hard, trying to imagine the hell that must have been.

"I got back there one more time and lifted the last man onto my shoulders. As I carried him, I could hear he was breathing, but not much else. Initially, I remember going down to my knees under his weight, but I must have gotten back up. Even now, I don't remember making it back to the building the last time, but I must have, because that's where we were reportedly found. And the rest you know. I must have blacked out, and I came to with the guys around me, Bottles dead and Stacks dying, and by some miracle, I had only a few scratches, probably from the last shell."

"You saved all their lives," Mario said, and Gordon shook his head.

"No. I was the one put in charge of the patrol and I got Bottles and Stacks killed. There's nothing that can make up for that. I should have been more vigilant watching the crowd. I should...." His voice trailed off.

Mario squeezed Gordon's hand. "You know you can't control everything, no matter how you try, and what happened there was as beyond your control as what happened to David. You didn't attack the market, but you did get your men out. That is all that matters." Gordon trembled, and Mario hugged him close as he began to cry. Mario knew he was finally truly mourning the loss of Bottles and Stacks. "It's all right. Let it out. You've held your grief and guilt inside for way too long."

Gordon clung to him, and Mario lightly stroked his lover's short hair, trying to provide comfort for something that Mario figured couldn't be easily comforted away. The self-doubt and guilt would stay with Gordon no matter what he said or did. Mario knew he didn't have the power to help wipe that away. Only time and maybe finding someone who could understand would do that. Mario continued holding Gordon until he straightened up and wiped his eyes with the back of his hand.

"It's okay to grieve," Mario said softly. "It's natural and healthy." Gordon nodded even though he didn't look convinced. "Trust me," Mario added.

"I'll try," Gordon said. "I suppose I should call the Navy agents and arrange to tell them what I remembered. They may not believe me, but I promised I'd call if I remembered anything." Gordon settled back on the sofa.

"I know you were worried about what you couldn't remember, but on some level you have to be relieved that what happened wasn't as bad as what you said the special agents insinuated," Mario said carefully. In his mind, Gordon was a hero. Yes, his two friends had died, but he'd saved the others' lives and gotten them out of harm's way. That made him a hero in Mario's book, regardless of what the Navy might think. "Call them in the morning and find out what they want to do. Get everything out into the open so you can deal with it. What the Navy thinks or believes is immaterial. It's what you think and how you deal with it that counts."

"You really believe that, don't you?" Gordon asked.

"Of course," Mario said. "I believe what you told me, and you have to learn to live with it. That's what counts. Whatever the Navy thinks will be recorded and forgotten in the bowels of government files that no one cares about. But you have to live with it, and from my perspective, you're a hero. You saved all their lives, and even though your friends died, you getting them out of there might have given them a chance if they hadn't been hurt so badly. I know it's hard, but concentrate on the good."

"How can I?" Gordon rasped.

"Did any of the men you got out have children?" Mario asked, and Gordon nodded, looking a bit skeptical. "Then think of those children. Because of what you did, they still have a father to hug after school and teach them to throw a baseball when they grow up. I know you're grieving for your friends and think you failed them, but you didn't, and if you let some of the guilt you're carrying go, you'll be able to see that."

"How?" Gordon asked.

"Only you can answer that. I can't tell you how you do it. That has to come from inside you, but I'll be here if you want to talk."

"But how can you be so sure I did the right thing? That I deserve to let go of the guilt?" Gordon asked, and Mario felt a small smile tug at his lips.

"Because I love you," Mario said with a shrug. "If you had made a mistake, it wouldn't change the way I feel about you. We're all human and we all make mistakes, but there's one thing I definitely know. You would never run from something you'd done wrong—you'd face it and accept the consequences. You did that when you first came here, and nothing in the time I've known you suggests you'd ever act any differently." Mario stared hard and strong into Gordon's eyes. "Sometimes guilt is deserved, but at other times, it's a waste, and in this case I'd think it's a waste. Would Bottles and Stacks want you to feel this way?" Mario knew he was probably being a bit devious, but whatever worked.

"No, they'd probably kick my ass," Gordon admitted.

"Then let it go. You're carrying something you don't need to," Mario said before standing up. "I'm going to check on the animals." He figured Gordon probably needed some time to think things over. "I won't be gone too long." Mario had stepped outside and started walking toward the barn when he heard brisk steps behind him. He knew it was Gordon, and when Gordon took his hand, they walked together toward the barn.

THREE days later, Mario paced the floor. Gordon was in town, meeting with the Naval commanders. "Screw it," Mario said, and he called the number he'd gotten out of Gordon's phone. "Mr. Greeves?" he asked when a man's voice answered.

"Who is this? How did you get this number?" They might have been framed as questions, but they sounded like demands and came fast.

Mario took a deep breath. "My name is Mario and I'm a friend of Gordon's. I need your help on his behalf."

"How so?" the man asked rather gruffly, but at least he didn't hang up.

"Gordon remembered what happened in the market and he's talking to the Navy people now. But he's having a tough time dealing with what happened. He was even before he remembered, and this doesn't seem to have helped."

"So the uniform dweebs found him. What does he need?" The tone was much more urgent and less gruff. "Is he in trouble?"

"I doubt it," Mario answered. "But what happened isn't my story to tell. I'm sure he will when the time comes. The thing is I think he needs to talk to someone who understands what he went through. I'm not talking about a shrink. He won't talk to them anyway. I'm hoping you might know of someone who has been through something like what Gordon has who would be willing to talk to him. He doesn't need a shrink, but...." Mario wasn't sure quite how to phrase it. "He needs another Marine who has been through the same hell he has and survived."

"We all went through hell, but yeah, I can see that." Greeves was quiet for a few seconds, and Mario waited impatiently. "I wouldn't let Gord tell me where he was, plausible deniability and all, but I don't think that matters now."

"He's at a ranch outside Jackson, Wyoming," Mario said. "I know it's a long shot, but I wasn't sure who else to call who might know people."

"I'll see what I can do," Greeves said. "I can't make promises, but I'll give it a try. I take it I can call you at this number."

"Yes, thank you," Mario said, and Greeves ended the call. Mario knew he'd done the right thing, but he wasn't sure if Gordon would agree, so he decided to wait and see if anything came of the call before saying anything. Jamming his phone back in his pocket, Mario left the house. As he walked toward the barn, he heard the whine of ATVs approaching.

"We have a fence break and wandering cattle," Haven called, and Mario got the men working near the ranch onto ATVs, along with himself, and they followed Haven.

Mario spent the rest of the day directing the repair of the fence while Haven rounded up the steers. It was nearly dark by the time the stragglers had been rounded up and put back where they belonged, and the men headed back to the ranch. Mario had been wondering how things had gone for Gordon for most of the day, and as he got closer to the ranch, his anxiety ramped up. He pulled his ATV into the equipment shed and turned off the engine.

"Everything okay?" Gordon asked as Mario climbed off.

"Yeah, fence break. Nothing to worry about," Mario added. "The posts in that section need to be replaced. We'll get the supplies ordered and do that in the next week." Mario walked over to where Gordon stood. "How did things go?"

Gordon huffed and turned around, striding toward the house. This was obviously something he didn't want to talk about in the open. Mario almost struggled to keep up with him. "The bastards already knew what I had to tell them!" Gordon spat once the door closed behind them. "I told them what I remembered, the hell I went through and what happened to my friends, and all the fuckers did was nod. They already knew. Hell, I'm sure the slippery bastards knew when they were here last time, but didn't say anything." Mario jumped when Gordon pounded his fist on the table. "The bastards knew!"

"What does it matter?" Mario asked. "So they knew. The important thing is that you remembered and you told them what you knew. Now they can go away and leave you in peace. You owe them nothing, and if they show up again, we'll kick them off the ranch. You've done your bit, and now they can sit and spin!" Mario held up his thumb and both men looked at each other before bursting into peals of laughter.

"Sit and spin," Gordon said, holding his side. "I'd like to see you tell them that." Gordon nearly fell on the floor, and Mario watched, his own laughter deriving from Gordon's mirthful abandon. He'd never seen him laugh like this, so freely, without care. "I had one of those when I was a kid. My friends and I used to see who could go the longest without puking." Gordon continued laughing.

"I bet you were the winner," Mario said, still smiling as his laughter died down.

"No, that was Bottles," Gordon said, and Mario stood still, watching as Gordon's laughter morphed into a cry of pain. Mario hadn't realized they had been childhood friends. In an instant, he was by Gordon's side, holding him.

"Why didn't you tell me?" Mario asked as he slowly rocked back and forth. 'I knew he was your buddy, your brother, but...." Mario couldn't speak any longer. The thought of everything that had happened and Gordon knowing Bottles since childhood wrenched Mario's heart.

"I guess I never really thought about it. He was always there, when we were kids and in high school. We signed up for the Corps together and requested the exact same type of training," Gordon explained through barely suppressed sobs. "We were separated in training anyway, and then reunited when we were sent to Iraq. By some miracle, we were placed in the same unit. Together again, and nothing felt better. He, Stacks, and I got closer than any brothers. We knew everything and shared everything."

"Did they know… about you?" Mario asked.

Gordon nodded slowly. "I told them eventually, and they both shrugged and life went on. Neither of them cared. Like I said, we were brothers and nothing could change that. Except the day they died." Gordon slumped against him, and Mario nearly sank to the floor. He managed to keep his feet and moved them both toward the sofa. He sank down onto it and brought Gordon with him.

"It's okay," Mario said softly. "You've been through a lot, and as I said before, it's okay to grieve." Mario could tell Gordon was still trying to control his emotions, but he was quickly losing the battle.

"What am I going to do without them?" Gordon asked.

"You'll go on, because life goes on. People enter and leave our lives," Mario explained.

"Will you leave?" Gordon asked quietly.

"No. I won't leave," Mario said, tilting Gordon's face to him before kissing him lightly. "I'm like a Marine, in it for the long haul. I don't give up, and I don't let go of what's mine. I held onto David for months after he left because I didn't want to let him go. Do you think I would hold onto you any less tightly?" Mario said, and Gordon shook his head, wrapping his arms around Mario's waist and resting his head on Mario's chest. "I'll hold you forever if you want me to."

Gordon nodded against his chest and made a positive sound without moving away or saying anything else. He and Gordon sat that way until Gordon finally got up, and they quietly went to bed, where Mario held Gordon all night long.

MARIO'S phone woke him in the morning. He heard it in the other room and carefully got out of bed to answer it. "I found someone who I think is able to talk to Gord." Mario recognized Greeves's voice. "I don't know how much good it will do, but he's willing to try."

"Thank you," Mario said.

"He'll be there today, I believe," Greeves said. "He's the uncle of one of the men Gordon helped in Iraq. He feels he owes Gordon a debt and he'll do whatever he can to help him. In fact, he may already know him, in a way." Greeves chuckled. "Tell Gord I'll call him soon." Greeves hung up, and Mario wondered exactly what he meant.

"Who was that?" Gordon asked from behind him, and Mario turned and took in his lover's godlike nakedness.

"Greeves. I called him a few days ago to see if he could find someone who could help you," Mario told him, and Gordon stalked toward him. "Don't be angry. I thought if you had someone who had been through something similar, he could tell you how he dealt with it, and I figured it had to be another Marine and not some shrink."

"What did Greeves say to that?" Gordon asked cautiously.

"He said he found the uncle of one of the men you saved who lives in the area. He'll stop by sometime today." Mario stepped backward as Gordon continued moving forward. "I was trying to help." Mario wasn't sure if Gordon was angry or not. "It's not going to hurt you to talk to someone who might understand."

"I know, but I don't know if it will help either," Gordon said. "Thank you."

Mario relaxed and let Gordon capture him. "But next time, tell me about it first. I don't really like surprises."

"I wasn't sure if it would work or if he could find someone he trusted to speak with you," Mario explained. "He also said that you may already know him. I don't know what he meant and he hung up before I could ask."

Gordon shook his head. "That's Greeves. He loves cloak-and-dagger stuff, watches every spy movie ever made. Whenever he can get away with it, Greeves loves to act mysterious. He usually can't pull it off, but this time it seems to have worked for him." Gordon took his hand and led Mario back down the hall toward the bedroom. "Greeves would never hurt me, so we'll let him have his fun, and we'll have ours before we have to go to work." Gordon chuckled as he pushed Mario onto the bed. Mario hadn't expected Gordon to be up for this, but then again, there were many types of healing.

THEY were both a little late for work, but they made up for it in energy. Wally proceeded to tease them both as he gathered his things to leave on a call. Gordon and Mario stopped for a quick lunch and then returned to work. There was plenty to do to get ready for winter, so everyone was busy, even though in the heat, winter was as far from everyone's minds as possible.

"Hey, Mario," Paul said as he hurried over to where Mario was working to fix part of the paddock fence. "There's someone here and he says he needs to see you." Paul looked nervous. Mario sighed, wondering what could be wrong now. After putting his tools away, he followed Paul around front and approached a man in what looked like a Marine uniform, perfectly pressed.

"Hello, I'm Mario, can I help you?"

The man turned around, and Mario nearly jumped back when he saw the sheriff staring back at him.

Chapter Eleven

GORDON heard Mario's voice in the yard and wandered out of the barn. He stopped when he saw the uniform and damn near saluted. It wasn't until he looked closer that he recognized the sheriff.

"Fisher," the sheriff said. Gordon began moving closer, and he saw Mario nod to him and walk away. "I understand we need to talk."

If this was the man Greeves had found for him to talk to, his first instinct was to say fuck it and continue like he had. Gordon didn't answer, just stared back, his gaze hard.

"I'm not here as the sheriff or the man you saw the other night. I'm here Marine to Marine and because of Benny Thomas—I believe you know him," the sheriff said, and Gordon nodded. "I understand he was one of the men you pulled out of that market."

"Yes," Gordon answered.

"He calls me Uncle Matt. So, kid, I owe you, and I'm here to try to help repay that debt."

"Fuck, it's a small world," Gordon said, and the sheriff motioned toward the paddock.

"Getting smaller every day," the sheriff told him, and he leaned against the paddock fence. Gordon joined him a little reluctantly.

"Sheriff, I…."

"Call me Matt," he said. "I was in the first Gulf War. In the wave of men that first crossed the border into the desert. I heard the sound of shells, guns, and explosions so loud you could feel them in deep in your bones. Got wounded and went back, because it's what we do."

"Yes. Marines don't run from the fire, we run toward it," Gordon said, repeating what had been drilled into them throughout his entire Marine life.

"So what's got you running now?" Matt asked.

"I'm not running. I'm trying to make sense of what happened," Gordon answered briskly, his anger bristling to the surface.

"No, you're running. Not in the conventional sense, but you are. I don't know what happened out there, and no one can unless they were there, but I lost friends in Desert Storm—good friends, brothers, just like you. It comes with being a Marine. The men we serve with are brothers, we rely on them, take care of them, and they watch out for us." Matt turned to him, his expression almost fierce. "You did your job. You looked out for your brothers, pulling all of them to safety."

Gordon wanted to turn away from the intensity in those blue eyes, but he held their gaze. "No, I didn't."

"Yes, you did. Your job was to patrol the market. You did that. There was no way you could have known it would be attacked the way it was. When your men were pinned down, you found a safe place and got all of them there, wounded, no less. So, yes, you did your job, and yes, you lost two of your closest friends because of it, and that's when you started running."

"I couldn't do it any longer," Gordon said.

"I know that. Every man has his limits, and there is no shame in admitting yours. You served long and hard, saving many civilian lives and the lives of your brothers again and again, just like they did for you. But understand me: reaching your limit does not mean you can run."

"I have not…," Gordon began and then stopped.

"See, you know you've been running. You got out and stayed away from everyone. You spent over a year wandering from town to town and place to place, sinking deeper and deeper into yourself. How do you think those eco people got to you, a Marine? You were so desperate you jumped at anything to survive." Matt paused, those eyes shining with energy.

"How do you know how I feel?" Gordon challenged.

"Because I did the exact same thing. When my last tour was over, I wanted nothing more than to be free, so I ran too, spent two years out here, most of it camping under the stars and living off the land. Loved it, but it didn't do me a fucking bit of good. All the problems I thought I'd left behind were still there waiting for me when I came to my senses. After all that time, I still saw the exact same thing whenever I closed my eyes. That hadn't changed, nor had my family and friends. You see, the only person I'd been running from was me." Matt curled his lips into a slight smile. "No one can change the past, not me and not you. What we can change is how we feel about it."

"But my friends are still dead. How can I change that they're not here and that I could have saved them?" Gordon asked, even though deep down he already knew the answer.

"You can't. But they were Marines and they deserve to be remembered as Marines. You can still grieve for them, but remember they died with honor, fighting for the country they loved and protecting civilian lives. They knew the risks just like you did, but they did their jobs and lived their lives proudly and to the fullest. Remember them for that, for what they did in life. Yes, they're dead, but they'll always be with you, just like a piece of every brother who ever put on this uniform is with you each and every day." Matt straightened up, standing perfectly tall, eyes forward, shoulders back, and Gordon did the exact same thing. "Honor them for being what and who they were. Not everyone can wear this uniform; not everyone is cut out for it. You were, they were—remember that and not the rest." Matt took a step back and whirled on one foot before striding across the yard.

"Did the dreams ever stop?" Gordon asked, and Matt stopped, turning around.

"No. Thank God. But they changed. Over time, they switched to show me what was really important, and they will for you too." A look of peaceful contentment washed over Matt's face. "You have to give it time and let the people around you share what you feel. Sometimes the hardest battles for us are the ones we have with our own feelings." Matt grinned. "Contrary to what we were taught, it is okay to have feelings and to share them with the people around us. Don't run from them—it'll be the biggest mistake you'll ever make." Matt turned back around and got into his car. He waved to Wally and to Dakota, who were watching him from the porch. Then he pulled down the drive and out onto the road.

Gordon watched and stood in place long after Matt had left.

"Are you going to kill me?" Mario asked from behind him. Gordon was about to turn around when he felt Mario slide his hands around his waist, pressing his chest to his back, resting his chin on his shoulder. "I hope he was able to help."

Gordon continued watching where Matt had gone. "I don't know if he helped or if he can help. He did make a good point, that I have been running from things and that I haven't been treating my friends' memory the way I should."

"How so?" Mario asked softly.

"They were Marines and they deserve to be remembered as Marines," Gordon answered with surprising calmness. "Maybe he did help," Gordon added when he realized there was none of the inner turmoil, rage, and shame that had swirled and boiled inside him all this time. He felt calm—still sad, but under control. The rest of what they talked about Gordon kept to himself. He wasn't going to relay their entire conversation to Mario. What they'd talked about was between them, and whether it actually helped in the long run or not was yet to be seen, but what stuck in his mind was that Mario had cared enough about him to make the effort to try to find someone to help. That meant more than the talk itself. Matt was right—it was okay to have feelings and to express them.

Gordon turned in Mario's embrace, pulling his lover and friend to him gently, carefully. When they came together, it was usually with such power and overarching need Gordon sometimes forgot there were other ways to do this. Slowly he moved his face closer to Mario's, bringing their lips together softly. "He reminded me of something important." Mario said nothing but his head tilted slightly to the side. "I want you to know that you mean a great deal to me. I don't say it often enough, and you've even had to goad me into expressing it, but this is all me. I love you, Mario, from the depths of my heart. There hasn't been and probably never will be another person who makes me feel the way you do. When I'm with you, the world seems right, and no matter what happens, I know you'll be there." Gordon hugged Mario tight. "I want you to know that I'll be there for you too. It may sound corny, but I'll hold you, care for you, love you, and cherish you until death do us part, if you'll let me."

Gordon lifted his head from Mario's shoulder and gazed into his eyes. They were filled with tears, and one ran down Mario's cheek. Gordon wiped it away. "David isn't such a bad guy, but he's still a fool because he could leave you. Maybe he's got more courage than I do, because that's something I could never bring myself to do."

"You big goof," Mario began, blinking hard. "You've been quiet about stuff like this the entire time I've known you, and now you say all these things and make me cry like some girl." Mario turned away, and Gordon gently touched his chin.

"You don't have to hide what you feel from me. I know I don't have to hide what I feel from you. Maybe that's the best part of all." Gordon knew Matt had been right. He had been running from a lot of things, and it was time to stop. He'd been afraid, and that fear had taken the form of a need to control everything he possibly could around him. Mario deserved better than that, and tonight after they'd finished their work and had dinner, Gordon was going to show Mario just how much he mattered to him.

They broke apart when a throat cleared loudly behind them. "I get back from a call and what do I see? You two making goo-goo eyes at each other."

"Dakota's inside—you can make goo-goo eyes at him if you're jealous," Gordon retorted, and Wally gaped for a few seconds before chuckling.

"Okay, but don't you have work to do?" Wally asked. They did, and they both sheepishly got back to it.

Gordon made sure he finished his work first. He got in his car and took off for town, stopping at the grocery store and managing to get everything he needed. Then he made a beeline back to the ranch and carried all the groceries into the house before beginning to cook. He felt like the chefs in one of those cooking shows on television.

Eventually, the salad was made and in the refrigerator. He'd found a recipe for a salad with pecans, various greens, strawberries, and a light, tangy dressing. All he needed to do was dress it and that was ready to go. The beef roast was in the oven and the scent filled the entire house. Gordon half expected the scent to burst out of the house and fill the ranch, leading to a line forming outside the door. Thankfully, everyone stayed away except Mario, who came inside as Gordon was steaming the vegetables and making the mashed potatoes. "Oh God, that smells good," Mario said, moving closer. He angled for a kiss, and Gordon turned off the burner before letting Mario tug him away and into his arms. "You did all this for me?"

"Of course," Gordon answered with a smile. "This is only the beginning. I have big plans for tonight, so I suggest you get cleaned up. Dinner will be ready in less than twenty minutes, and I want everything to be hot when we sit down, including you." Gordon cupped Mario's cheeks, kissed him hard, and then stepped back, waiting for him to leave the room so he could breathe again and return to making dinner.

Gordon had the salads plated and the food ready to serve by the time Mario returned with his hair still wet. Gordon wasn't sure what smelled better—the food or Mario, when he got another kiss. He decided he'd eat food now and save dessert for later. They both sat down and began to eat.

"God, this is amazing," Mario said as he ate the salad. They were both hungry, so that didn't last long, and soon they were digging in to the rest of the meal. Gordon was used to eating big in the Marines, but the ranch work built an even larger appetite. They talked some, kissed some, touching each other, but mostly they were ravenous. "This is amazing," Mario told him as he ate his third piece of beef.

"Thank you. I love to cook, and I love people who eat." Not that he was lacking in that department either.

"I know. It's one of the things I like about you. Whatever you do, you throw yourself into it." Mario swallowed another bite and set his fork on the table. "I talked to David today, and he's doing better all the time. The doctors want him to go to therapy to make sure everything heals correctly, but he's going to be fine." Mario's expression changed slightly. "Did it really go okay today? I mean, your talk with the sheriff."

"I knew what you meant," Gordon answered. "And yeah, I think it went okay. He went through a lot of the same things I did. It's hard to explain, but I think I'm going to be okay." Maybe it was all about how a person thought about things.

Their conversation changed again, much to Gordon's gratitude, and they finished the meal speaking of happier things. "I'll help with the dishes," Mario said as he helped clear the table.

"Most things are in the dishwasher. I just need to put things away and then we're all set." Gordon began getting out plastic containers for the leftovers, and Mario rinsed the dishes before placing them into the dishwasher. Working together, they were done in no time, and after turning out the kitchen lights, they retired to the living room. Mario found a movie and they started watching. Gordon wasn't paying attention to it and soon leaned over to kiss Mario. That kiss led to another, and soon he had Mario on the sofa, legs dangling to the floor, shirt up under his arms while Gordon lavishly kissed and sucked his skin. Mario moaned steadily, and Gordon smiled against his lover's skin. Gordon tugged off Mario's shirt before pulling off his own. "You're an incredible man," Gordon told Mario before kissing him hard, sucking on his lips as their tongues dueled in war of love. Winning wasn't the objective here.

"Maybe we should move someplace more comfortable," Gordon suggested as he reached over and turned off the television. Then he climbed off Mario and extended a hand, tugging him to his feet. Without letting go, he led Mario down the hall to the bedroom, closing the door behind them. Alone—they were alone, and Mario was all his.

Slowly he pulled them together, engulfing Mario in his arms as he brought their lips together. "I love you," Gordon said softly once he broke the kiss. He remembered in the Corps when guys would be on the phone to their wives, and he knew they were being told they were loved because the guy would always go beet red and then say the words back, but rather softly, in case the other guys heard. Well, Gordon was prepared to shout it from the rooftop if need be. No more hiding or being quiet about it.

"I love you too," Mario told him. Gordon had never realized how important or special those words could be until they came from Mario. Gordon held him tight and wasn't about to let him go anytime soon. Stroking Mario's back with one hand, he used the other to open Mario's belt and jeans until they slid down his legs.

Mario stepped out of them, and Gordon maneuvered him onto the bed. Mario chuckled as they bounced, and Gordon cut him off with a kiss.

"I want you to know how much you mean to me," Gordon said to Mario, their gazes meeting intently.

"I already know," Mario replied. "I've known for a while. Your actions, the way you look at me, the way you touch me, told me how you felt long before you said the words." Mario kissed him as he worked the waistband of his pants. Soon Mario slid them down his legs, and Gordon kicked them off. Their underwear followed between kisses and touches.

Backs arched, mouths explored, and moans filled the room as they made love, slowly, lovingly, driving each other higher and higher up a mountain of passion. Mario wrapped his legs around Gordon's waist, groaning deeply when their bodies joined in a searing blaze of passion. But contrary to their usual coupling, Gordon took his time, moving deeply and slowly.

"Please, Gordon," Mario begged softly.

Determined to take his time, Gordon gently stilled Mario's urgent motions, kissing him as he continued his deliberate movement inside his lover's body. "I want you to feel me tomorrow and the next day," Gordon said, stopping as Mario groaned his frustration. "I want you to always know who loves you, who cares for you, and"—Gordon snapped his hips, burying himself deep in Mario's heat—"who is the only person who can make your eyes roll to the back of your head and steal your breath away. Because you steal mine at least once each and every day." Where these flowery words were coming from, Gordon had no idea. He'd never been a romantic person, but he had to tell Mario what was in his heart.

Mario gasped and swallowed hard, gripping the bedding, and Gordon slowly withdrew completely and then pressed back inside, to Mario's long, deep groan. "I love you too, now please...."

Gordon gave his lover what he wanted, driving them higher and higher, filling the room with whimpers and moans that burst out the open window and floated over the land.

"I love you," Mario cried when his passion became too much, and Gordon watched in wondered awe as he blissfully came, painting his chest with streaks of white, eyes wide with wonder.

Watching Mario's release was nearly overwhelming, but Gordon kept himself together and waited until Mario rejoined him before slowly moving inside his lover once again. As he leaned forward, their lips met, and Gordon felt his own release building. "I love you so much," Gordon said, barely above a whisper. Now that he had found a voice for his feelings, it seemed like a dam had opened and he had to tell Mario. His release got closer and closer, becoming more difficult to contain with each fraction of a second.

"You mean the world to me," Mario told him, reaching up to stroke his cheek. Gordon clamped his eyes closed as his entire body tingled and he let go, his release overtaking him in a blinding flash.

Gordon rode the waves of pleasure until he could hold out no longer. Holding Mario tight, Gordon caught his breath. With a small moan from each of them, their bodies separated, and Mario rolled him onto his back. Gordon was still catching his breath when he felt Mario leave the bed and return a few moments later. Mario quickly and efficiently cleaned them up. He left and then quickly returned, climbing back into bed.

They were both quiet as Gordon pulled Mario close. "I love listening to the night," he confessed. "I used to do that when it was quiet in the desert, but this is so different," Gordon said. "That always sounded strange, but this sounds"—he held Mario tighter—"and feels like home."

Epilogue

MARIO drove as Gordon slept in the passenger seat. As he'd found over the past few days, Gordon could sleep anywhere, and at the drop of a hat, it seemed. Driving to Cheyenne, flying on a plane to Washington, DC, and then taking a plane back, all within two days, had been enough to wipe both of them out, and Mario wished he shared Gordon's ability to sleep anywhere.

"Where are we?" Gordon asked, sliding his eyes open.

"Little over an hour from the ranch. You slept most of the drive from Cheyenne," Mario said, stifling a yawn. He'd been driving for a while, and the travel and excitement over the past few days was catching up with him.

"Pull over and I'll drive for a while. You know we could have spent the night in Cheyenne and driven back in the morning," Gordon added, and Mario pulled off the road, grateful for a rest.

"Then we'd miss the barbeque," Mario said, yawning before he unhooked his seat belt and got out of the car. He walked around the back and climbed into the passenger seat. After fastening his seat belt, he waited until Gordon was done adjusting everything to fit him, and then they were off again. Mario closed his eyes and tried to sleep, but the seat was uncomfortable and he was just excited enough about the past few days and the party waiting for them back at the ranch. Dakota hadn't had one of these since his father passed away, and Mario was thrilled he was doing one again. When they had to make a trip to DC, Mario had promised that they would be back in time if at all possible.

"Rest," Gordon told him and reached around, pulling out a pillow from behind the seat. "This should help." Mario had forgotten, and soon he was reasonably comfortable and closed his eyes, shutting his mind down for a while and letting Gordon drive.

Mario woke when the sound under the tires changed. They were passing just outside town and were minutes from the ranch. The sun would be setting in an hour and the party would be in full swing by the time they arrived, but they would make it. Gordon drove the last few miles as Mario's fatigue vanished.

The ranch drive was packed with cars along both sides. Gordon maneuvered around the side, parking near their house. Mario heard him sigh. "You know everyone is going to make a big deal out of things," Gordon said quietly without opening his door. "That's not what I want. This came at a cost, and...."

"What would your friends do if they were here?" Mario asked.

Gordon smiled and turned to his lover. "They'd probably take me out to get drunk beyond belief. They would have, too. Their celebration would probably have put everything they'd ever done to date to shame."

"Then you owe it to them to celebrate." Mario leaned over the seat and lightly touched his cheek. "This is your celebration, and everyone you know is waiting to see you."

"Have you told them?" Gordon asked.

"No, it's your news to tell, not mine, but remember how they would want you to act," Mario said, looking at Gordon with as much pride as he'd ever felt in his life. "They'd want you to be proud. You saved many lives that day," Mario said. "I never met the friends you lost, but I bet, if they're anything like you, they're looking down and smiling right about now, because you would be."

Gordon seemed to think about it for a few seconds and then nodded once before opening the door. "I don't want this to be a big topic of conversation. Okay?" Gordon said, and Mario agreed before he too got out of the truck.

The party was indeed going strong. Multiple voices intermingled with music and laughter, and the scent of food mixed with the usual smells of the ranch. "Just follow your nose," Mario told Gordon when he looked like he wasn't quite sure what to do. They easily found the buffet and filled their plates. On their way to find people they knew, they passed groups of kids playing games under the lights and passed many conversation groups of adults laughing and talking.

"You made it," Wally called, hurrying over to give them both a hug. Dakota wasn't far behind, looking indulgently at his lover.

"I think you've had enough beer," Dakota told Wally, lifting the cup out of his hand.

"I have not," Wally protested and then proceeded to hiccup multiple times in quick succession. "Okay, maybe I have." The smile on his face didn't diminish, though. "We were beginning to wonder if you were going to get back in time. How was your trip?"

"Long. Very long," Gordon answered with surprisingly little excitement.

"There are tables set up near the bonfire if you want to join us there," Dakota explained and pointed. "You can also take your plates and go inside if you're tired. It won't be quiet, but at least you'll be alone if that's what you'd rather do." Dakota looked Gordon square in the face, and Mario knew that was for Gordon's benefit. He also knew Gordon was seriously considering taking him up on the offer.

"Thanks," Gordon said. "It's just a lot of flying and driving. We'll have a seat and eat."

"Good." Dakota clapped Gordon on the shoulder. "Beer's in the keg, and there's also soda and water. Help yourself to whatever you'd like. The special entertainment will start shortly." Dakota hurried off, but Wally followed them to the table.

"Did everything go okay?" Wally asked once they'd sat down. "You know you can't keep a secret around here, at least not that kind of secret."

"You know?" Gordon asked, and Wally nodded. Mario watched Gordon shrug and then begin eating. "It's no big deal," Gordon said between bites, barely looking up from his plate.

Even in the dim light, Mario saw Wally's eyes widen in surprise. Mario shrugged and shook his head slightly. It was a big deal, even if Gordon didn't believe it now. In some ways, Mario understood how Gordon felt, but in others he had no idea. The man was still a bit of a mystery and probably would be for the rest of their lives together. Wally alternately looked at both of them and then quietly stood up and walked away from the table. Mario watched him walk away.

"IF YOU think Wally is going to leave this alone, you're nuts," Mario told Gordon.

"He wouldn't," Gordon said as he paused, fork halfway to his mouth.

"It's Wally. Of course he would, and you know he probably will. So be happy your friends will be happy for you," Mario told him, and Gordon growled softly. Mario chuckled. "Remember you can't control everything, and there are worse things than your friends being happy and proud of you. Bottles and Stacks would be proud, so let your current friends be proud." Gordon growled again, only softer this time. "At least smile."

Gordon swallowed his bite of food and sighed softly. "I just don't feel like I deserve it. Not for this," Gordon said. "I just did it without thinking."

"Then that's exactly why you deserve it, because you acted based on what was in your heart."

"Good evening, everyone." Dakota's raised voice cut off further conversation. "I want to thank everyone for coming. It's been both a difficult and rewarding few years. This is the first one of these we've had without my dad, and I think he'd be pleased we're having them again." Everyone applauded loudly, and Dakota waited until the sound died before continuing. "We've also had a bit of excitement lately, and I'm pleased to report that the eco group that threatened this ranch, and a few others, has been caught and the members are in jail awaiting trial. Also thanks to two of our own, a source of illicit drugs and crime in our area has been put out of business." Dakota looked at David and then over where they sat, but Gordon tried his best to ignore it.

"Now with all that said, I'll shut up." People applauded. "But first I have to tell you"—a few teasing groans floated through the crowd—"that one of our neighbors has agreed to sing a few songs for you tonight." Dakota sat down, and Mario watched as Wilson, also known as Willie Meadows, carried his guitar up near the fire. Mario finished the last of his dinner and threw away his plate before grabbing Gordon's hand so they could move closer to listen. Benches and chairs ringed the relatively small fire, which they only needed for light, certainly not heat. Mario found two places on one of the benches, and they sat down to listen.

Willie placed his guitar on his lap and began to play. He sang some old cowboy ballads, like "Don't Fence Me In," that everyone knew and sang along with. Mario leaned contentedly against Gordon and listened to the deep mellow voice, relaxing with each passing second. Then Willie sang two of his own songs before accepting everyone's applause and standing up, ostensibly to signal that he was done for the evening. Mario saw Wally hurry up to him, whispering into Wilson's ear. He nodded and without sitting down, brought the guitar up and began playing the Marine Hymn, walking through the crowd to where Mario and Gordon sat. Mario stood up, and so did Wally, Dakota, and Paul. Soon, others had joined them until everyone at the party stood.

Mario watched Gordon stand as well, staring at Willie as he came closer. Once the hymn was over, everyone applauded and remained standing. "I understand that one of our number just got back from Washington," Willie began. "Now, I understand that our little impromptu ceremony isn't much compared to what I'm sure is involved when the Marine Corps awards a Silver Star, but it comes from the heart." Small gasps and murmurs went up from the gathering. Willie stood in front of Gordon, shaking his hand. "Thanks for your service. You are a hero, to me and to all of us," Willie said. Gordon nodded and mumbled a thank-you. Willie nodded back, releasing Gordon's hand before moving away.

Mario moved closer, placing an arm around Gordon's waist. Yes, the ceremony at the ranch had been nothing like the one in Washington—no pomp, no military ceremony, no guns being shot in tribute—but during the entire event in Washington, not once had Gordon had tears in his eyes.

ANDREW GREY grew up in western Michigan with a father who loved to tell stories and a mother who loved to read them. Since then he has lived throughout the country and traveled throughout the world. He has a master's degree from the University of Wisconsin-Milwaukee and works in information systems for a large corporation. Andrew's hobbies include collecting antiques, gardening, and leaving his dirty dishes anywhere but in the sink (particularly when writing). He considers himself blessed with an accepting family, fantastic friends, and the world's most supportive and loving partner. Andrew currently lives in beautiful historic Carlisle, Pennsylvania.

Visit Andrew's website at http://www.andrewgreybooks.com and blog at http://andrewgreybooks.livejournal.com/. E-mail him at andrewgrey@comcast.net.

Also from ANDREW GREY

AN ISOLATED *Range*

ANDREW GREY

http://www.dreamspinnerpress.com

The RANGE Stories

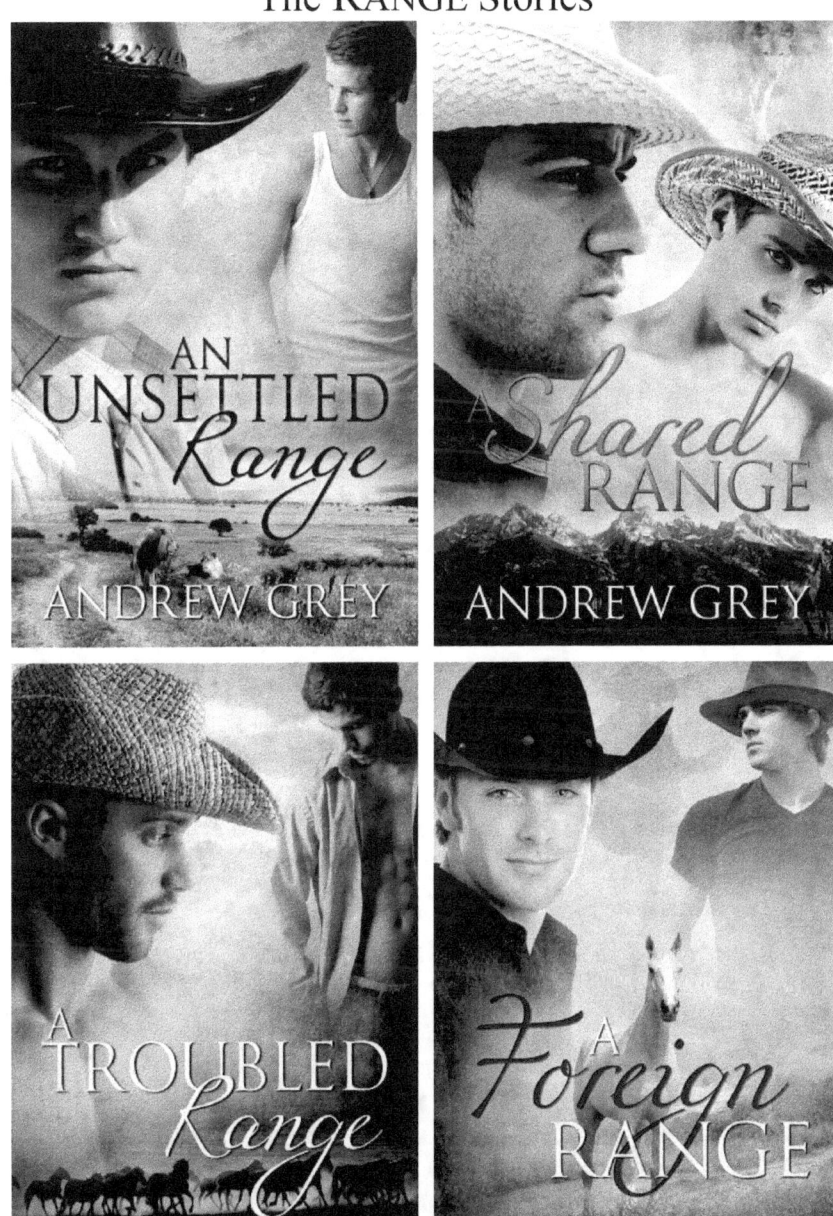

The ART stories

Now in Spanish, French, and Italian

www.ingramcontent.com/pod-product-compliance
Lightning Source LLC
Chambersburg PA
CBHW071007280626
47160CB00015B/1690